A Candlelight Ecstasy Romance™

"COME TO ME. BE MY MISTRESS. I'LL PROTECT YOU WITH MY LIFE. . . ."

"Your life but not your name," she blurted, her eyes shimmering with unshed tears.

"I told you why. I couldn't live if I found you were unfaithful to me."

"I could be unfaithful in spite of not being married," she said resentfully.

"I would see that you weren't. It's never the same."

His head lowered; his mouth parted to take her lips, but she wrenched herself away.

"Stop!" she cried.

But he clamped his lips over her mouth and enfolded her trembling body, forcing her to respond. Relentlessly he trailed kisses along the smooth skin of her neck, determined to bend her to his will. . .

CANDLELIGHT ECSTASY ROMANCES™

IMPETUOUS SURROGATE

Alice Morgan

A CANDLELIGHT ECSTASY ROMANCE ™

Published by
Dell Publishing Co., Inc.
1 Dag Hammarskjold Plaza
New York, New York 10017

Dell ® TM 681510, Dell Publishing Co., Inc.
Candlelight Ecstasy Romance™ is a trademark of
Dell Publishing Co., Inc.,
New York, New York.

ISBN: 0–440–14169–9

Printed in the United States of America

First printing—July 1982

Dear Reader:

In response to your continued enthusiasm for Candlelight Ecstasy Romances™, we are increasing the number of new titles from four to six per month.

We are delighted to present sensuous novels set in America, depicting modern American men and women as they confront the provocative problems of modern relationships.

Throughout the history of the Candlelight line, Dell has tried to maintain a high standard of excellence, to give you the finest in reading enjoyment. That is now and will remain our most ardent ambition.

Anne Gisonny
Editor
Candlelight Romances

CHAPTER ONE

"Your place or mine?" Alan coaxed tentatively, his breath hot on De-Ann's neck.

Embarrassed by his amorous attention, she glanced surreptitiously around the room to assure herself that they had not been observed. Drawing away from his annoying lips touching her neck, she glared at him. Disapproval darkened her eyes to a deep jade, a warning he had gone too far.

"Quit it, Alan," she whispered angrily, fearing his blatant question might have been overheard in the muted atmosphere of the elegant restaurant. "You know I don't care for you that way."

Undaunted by De-Ann's obvious irritation, Alan scooted closer against the plush velvet of the high-back booth and gripped her with surprising strength. Her shoulders, bared in a décolleté evening gown, felt so smooth and satiny beneath his hands, his emotions were heightened to the breaking point.

"My God, De-Ann, can't you see you're driving me mad?" he groaned in frustration, liquor loosening his tongue. His pale blue eyes dilated with sexual awareness as he looked at her long lustrous auburn hair, caught in the seductive overhead lighting of an elegant dining room in the heart of San Francisco. Its vibrant color glinted with an aureole of fire. Its heady fragrance drew him like magic.

Alan pulled back, letting his eyes rest on the beauty of De-Ann's heart-shaped face. Her thin brows arched in inquiry at his intense stare. Deep green eyes expressed each mood change, unless concealed by their fringe of thick black lashes. Her mouth never failed to excite him, its soft red fullness made for a man's lips. She turned away, her small straight nose profiled in perfect clarity.

His eyes were drawn to the curve of her slender throat and downward. The deeply shadowed cleft between the swell of her high firm breasts caused perspiration to bead on his brow. She was the most sensual woman he had ever seen. Just thinking about her wreaked havoc with his pulse rate. His grip tightened as he leaned forward.

"Don't hold me off again tonight, De-Ann . . . please." His voice raised. Anguish and frustration from her sexual indifference had shattered his limited control. His pleading words, spoken against her neck, carried beyond their table unintentionally. "I'm losing my mind, I want you so bad. Let's go to my place. We'd be dynamite together in bed."

"Okay—" De-Ann began before she was interrupted by the approach of a couple. She was unable to finish explaining that she was leaving—alone!

Squirming uncomfortably, she glanced upward, eyes locking with those of a stranger. For a brief moment he paused, his right arm clasped tightly by a sophisticated blond woman. He looked from De-Ann to Alan, his piercing eyes raking the man contemptuously with surprised recognition rather than disgust. A deep frown brought his brows together. Smiling cynically, he guided his companion across the room to their waiting table.

De-Ann glared at his retreating back, disturbed by the brooding, critical fierceness of his cobalt-blue eyes. Their curiosity changed to scorn when he observed Alan nuzzle her neck. Alan was so aroused, he was unaware he and De-Ann had had an audience.

Chin tilted defiantly, De-Ann withdrew, shrugging from Alan's clasp. Easing her hips a respectable distance away, she scolded her date beneath her breath, her eyes glinting with fury.

"Alan Anderson, if you don't keep your hands off me and your unwelcome verbal advances from our conversation, I'll walk out on you this instant!"

Chastised by her stormy temper, Alan sat back. After an apologetic look he smoothed the gleaming waves of his blond hair. Straightening his silk tie, he agreed reluctantly to cool his ardor. He looked at her, holding one hand up.

"Pax?"

Agreeing, she nodded, aware of the vast amount of alcohol they both had consumed during the long evening hours. Though sympathetic to his frustration, she remained adamant in her refusal to be coerced into his bed. Alan's occasional company the last few months had been enjoyable: he was a pleasant acquaintance when he didn't drink to excess. His wit, plus his ability to bear no grudge at her refusal to sleep with him, had made him an undemanding companion.

De-Ann sensed she was being watched and glanced covertly beneath her lashes across the room. Her nerves tensed involuntarily when she found the stranger staring at her, his expression arrogant, his strong jaw set in a firm line, as his eyes raked her figure. Irritated by the sensual awareness he aroused in her, she fought to obtain a modicum of composure.

Alan, noticing De-Ann's distraction, followed her gaze. Nodding in recognition, he leaned forward. "I see you've spotted the big man around town." He reached for a chilled bottle, wanting another glass of vintage champagne. "Big man, all right. But not big enough to father an heir to the Howell empire in the normal way." He laughed mysteriously. "Too inhibiting to his adventurous life-style, he claims." Alan swallowed the contents of his refilled glass in one gulp.

De-Ann was appalled by Alan's continued consumption of liquor yet interested in his story, so she sat still, looking at him with consternation. The indulged son of a prominent attorney, Alan had just passed his bar exam and would soon join his father as a junior partner. His smooth, handsome features, fair hair, and light eyes were spoiled by the occasional petulant droop of his mouth. Until that evening his actions had never been offensive.

De-Ann's eyes flitted nervously, a strange compulsion making her glance across the room again. Her chin raised defiantly toward the censuring face before she willfully reached for her glass. Her heart hammered at his thoughtful look. Annoyed that the stranger's gaze disturbed her, she forced her mind to quell her unsettled emotions.

She returned his stare, her actions openly rebellious. She consumed her effervescent drink haughtily, immediately handing her glass to Alan for refilling. Flirting outrageously, she sipped the contents with a sudden need for its end effect.

Stunned by De-Ann's changing personality, Alan readily complied. He reached for her hand, letting his fingers trail across the smooth skin of her wrist. His expression was smug, confidence glimmered in his eyes.

"I know something about our frowning friend that only one other living soul knows, De-Ann," he confided to her under his breath.

12

Despite a growing curiosity, she withdrew her hand from his clasp in order to stop his confidences. Just then the band burst forth with a loud pulsating beat that fit her sudden feeling of recklessness.

"Let's dance, Alan."

Eager to hold her shapely body, Alan stood, anxiously reaching for her shoulders. Excited by her touch, he trembled as she glided smoothly into his arms. Alan was an expert dancer, light on his feet, his mannerisms flamboyant. His golden hair and tall, graceful carriage as they swept around the floor soon drew several pairs of envious eyes. Attention remained riveted on the bewitching loveliness of the laughing girl in his arms. No eyes were as keen as those of the dark, intense man with the blond companion.

Wavy hair swaying around De-Ann's shoulders drew attention to her exposed spine. Her narrow waist and rounded hips were outlined in the clinging silk of a backless green dress. The knee-length skirt swirled around her long shapely legs, shown to advantage in spike-heel evening sandals.

De-Ann, shaken by the strangers continued sardonic observation, made no move to stop Alan as he spread his fingers over her back. She let him run his hands intimately up and down the expanse of creamy smooth skin as she smiled invitingly. Filled with confidence, he swept around the floor until he was stopped by other dancers next to his acquaintance, whose forceful personality beckoned De-Ann.

A sideways glance showed the man's teak-bronze face in explicit detail. His eyes were sharp as they scanned her from head to toe with the thoroughness of a practiced womanizer before he gave her a cynical smile, one brow raised in amusement.

Hard, irregular features, rough-cut raven-black hair,

and low sideburns contrasted vividly with the other softer, less masculine appearing men in the room. His brawny size, even when he was seated, was overpowering and commanded immediate attention. He wore his black evening suit and ruffled white shirt with casual confidence, the feminine frills not detracting from his blatant masculinity. Conversing nonchalantly with his attentive partner, he appeared uncaring that her eyes openingly invited, expressed a glowing willingness to satisfy any of his desires.

De-Ann shivered at his virile maleness, feeling a sudden dryness in her throat despite her numerous glasses of champagne. Unlike Alan, whose features were smooth and polished, he looked ruthless. Power and authority emanated from him as if part of his every breath. His broad shoulders moved as he leaned forward. De-Ann missed a step as she watched warily. She knew beneath the formality of his attire there would be steel-hard muscles, rippling flesh smooth to a woman's sensitive fingertips, a well-sculpted torso she suddenly longed to caress and explore.

Momentarily stunned by her unaccustomed surgence of sensual interest, De-Ann deliberately leaned into Alan. She let her fingers cling below the well-groomed hair on the nape of his neck.

Thrilled by De-Ann's attentiveness, Alan pulled her intimately close, his breath increasing as her curvaceous figure pressed against his harder contours. After the lengthy song ended, he gripped her waist and possessively guided her back to their table.

Disturbed by her intimate thoughts toward the compelling stranger, De-Ann agreed without hesitation to Alan filling her glass. He gloated, assuming she was suddenly agreeable to his earlier proposition.

"Who—who is that man, Alan?" De-Ann asked before emptying her glass of the cool sparkling liquid.

"Derek Howell. You've heard of him, of course?"

"A little. Our social circles don't mingle, I'm afraid," she murmured softly, raising her arms to briefly lift the weight of thick hair off her nape. Suddenly too warm, she wished she had eaten more of the excellently prepared meal, feeling a queasiness in her stomach followed by momentary dizziness.

"Order me a screwdriver please, Alan. This champagne is making my mouth dry," she requested huskily, moistening her lips with the tip of her tongue.

She was unaware of Alan's eyes glittering with desire and anticipation, or the feeling of victory her uninhibited response on the dance floor had given him. He ordered two drinks, then watched her expectantly until the cocktail waitress placed them on the table. Leaning forward, Alan fondled De-Ann's wrist as she let it rest on the table between them. He stroked the fine skin slowly.

"He's the well-known owner of Hidden Coves, north of here. The millionaires' playground on the California coast," Alan confided earnestly. "A development of second homes that are more sumptuous than most affluent persons' main residence."

De-Ann recalled reading of the well-publicized land development and seeing a layout in their brochure. She remembered it was breathtakingly beautiful, blending perfectly with the natural environment. "He looks too young to have acquired so much. Did he inherit?"

"He's not that young. Five years older than me, which makes him about thirty-six. He inherited the wealth, all right. His family line is prominent and pure blue blood, but the coastal project was financed through his own shrewd business sense. According to Dad, he's sharp as a tack and totally ruthless in his business dealings."

15

"Dishonest, you mean?"

"Not in the least. Astute, ingenious, and bold enough to back his hunches with all his resources. He refused to touch his inheritance until he had proved to himself he could survive by his skill and intelligence. That brawny build and tanned face come from hard work. He's a builder par excellence and can work rings around any of his men, which he often does."

"I've heard more about his affairs with women than of his physical talents as a builder," she mused, sipping the last of her drink. Annoyed by the mussy feeling in her head, she continued. "My secretary reads all the local gossip, and I've often heard her dreamy sighs when talking about him. I've never paid much interest other than remembering he's quite a ladies' man."

Alan leaned forward, whispering confidentially, "Oh, he's a ladies' man, all right. Dad knows him well. He told me that Derek's mother divorced his father when Derek was a little kid. She's supposed to have run off with some titled latin Romeo. Both were killed in a plane crash a few years later. His father's second wife tried to seduce him when he was fourteen. Derek was a cynic by sixteen when his old man's third wife made his life such hell, it forced him to move from the family mansion."

"How do you know so much, Alan? I wouldn't think his life-style or family problems would interest you," she asked, unaware that Alan was smugly enjoying her undivided attention as she listened to each word.

"He's been Dad's client for years." Alan's fair complexion flushing, he looked over the soft feminine curves of De-Ann. "Actually, I have always envied his success with women. His disdainful attitude seems to turn women on. I—I become too intense. Look at our relationship. I've been trailing after you for six months, but a lot of good it's done me. I've pleaded, cajoled, and charmed to no avail.

16

You rarely even let me . . . kiss you." Alan leaned forward, emphasizing each word jealously. "That husky brute would have had you in his bed the first night. Probably made you enjoy every minute too!"

Disturbed by the image of a night in Derek Howell's bed, De-Ann's heartbeat increased with alarm. Withdrawing her hand from Alan's clasp, she swallowed nervously.

"Hey, don't cool down now," he objected petulantly. "This is the most receptive you've ever acted toward me. I assumed you had changed your mind about . . . you know?"

"I didn't intend to encourage you, Alan. I am not going to bed with you and that's final!" she stated adamantly, her glorious eyes flashing with sparks of unconcealed temper.

Alan drew back, hands raised. "Okay, okay," he agreed quickly, though not entirely convinced she was sincere. "Dad doesn't want me to marry until I'm thirty-five anyway, though I might be tempted to defy him if you need a wedding ring before playing house."

Unaware of his boyish behavior for a thirty-one-year-old man, Alan pouted as De-Ann laughed softly. "You're priceless. If that was a proposal, it's an insult. Fortunately for you and your father I'm happy with my career. My business is profitable now but, as you know, very time consuming. I can't see your vanity putting up with my occupation just to get me into your bed." Her expression became serious. "The only reason I'd want to marry is to have a family."

"Why bother? You should do what Derek is going to do." Alan's eyes shifted toward the object of his conversation before he leaned toward De-Ann, whispering, "That brute needs an heir, yet he absolutely refuses to give up his single status. He's contracted Dad to find him a surrogate mother."

17

"What?" De-Ann exclaimed, astonished by his remark.

"You heard me. Derek feels it's necessary he beget an heir to continue the family name and inherit his fortune. He asked Dad to discreetly solicit a surrogate mother to have his offspring. He wants a healthy, bright woman. Young, but sensible enough to fill his demands without becoming maudlin or emotional over her child. If he finds a compatible female willing to bear his child, he'll pay all expenses and give her a sum of thirty thousand dollars. That's over three thousand a month. It'll be a planting through artificial insemination, yet."

"That's . . . immoral! Illegal, anyway," De-Ann blurted out.

"Not so. Dad's researched it and has prepared a lengthy opinion, though the California State Bar has just begun preliminary studies of the possible need for legislation. Dad feels the contract is legal. Since it will be Derek's own son or daughter, he won't even have to go through adoption proceedings. A petition to the court for permanent sole custody is adequate. It will all be done with the utmost secrecy so that the woman will never know who the donor is. She just carries the child, delivers, signs over all rights, collects her money, and continues on about her affairs a rich woman minus one squalling brat."

Aghast at Alan's statements, De-Ann raised her face. Her fiery eyes glared hatefully at Derek Howell, willing him to look up. She shuddered with dislike of his unconventional attitude, angered further as he returned her look with aloof disdain, one dark brow raised in question. "Someone should teach him a lesson . . . the monster." She tossed her head back angrily, hissing, "That's selling your own baby."

"You're wrong. There is no baby when the contract is drawn. Dad feels the fee is for agreement to terminate parental rights rather than procurement of a child."

18

"Don't nitpick, Alan," De-Ann grumbled. "Imagine thinking a woman would be willing to hand over her child like so much trash!"

"Don't be so naive, De-Ann," Alan scolded wryly, before leaning back in the booth. "This procedure is not as uncommon as you might think nowadays. Not every woman has a strong maternal streak, but I have yet to meet one who wouldn't enjoy earning a small fortune for nine months effort."

"My God, Alan . . . you're as bad as he is," she blurted out with scorn, her eyes darkening to gleaming jade as she straightened her shoulders in anger. "I can't imagine anything as cold-blooded as that arrangement for bearing babies. What about the poor child?"

"Poor child! You must be kidding. The kid will be born with a gold spoon in his mouth. It will have the best of everything. Derek owns a fabulous mansion in this city, a luxurious country home on his development, and travels worldwide like most people commute to work. His kid will want for nothing."

"Nothing but a mother's breast and tender arms."

"Neither of which Derek had or appears to have missed. Wake up to this century, De-Ann. Motherhood has become something most women indulge in for all the wrong reasons. It's used to hook a single man that's careless, keep a faltering marriage together, or please frustrated relatives that want to be grandparents. Look around you. How many of your friends take care of their own children or even seem to like the brats overmuch?"

Deep in thought, De-Ann was forced to admit there was some truth to Alan's statements. Most of her friends didn't seem to want to bother with caring for their children and complained constantly about the problems they caused.

"My mother," she said, smiling as she remembered her

19

loving parent. "Her adult life was wrapped up in my dad and me. Mom's the perfect example of motherhood." Meeting Alan's gaze, she added thoughtfully, "My secretary also seems indulgent to her family, though she has to work to make ends meet."

"That's two. Only two, and you know dozens of couples," he reminded her unnecessarily. "What about you? You're twenty-six with no apparent plans for motherhood that I know of."

Alan's words hit De-Ann hard. They forced her to admit she had shrugged aside any desire to marry; she had refused several offers from decent men. Intent on her own future, independent, and energetic, she had suppressed all desire for children through fulfillment in her work.

Suddenly depressed and introspective, she frowned, blaming it on the excess alcohol. "Take me home, Alan. I feel kind of sick." Rising to her feet, she felt dizzy, knowing she had been too indulgent when Alan plied her with liquor. In fact she felt decidedly light-headed. She swayed, before giggling in a deep throaty laugh.

"I think I'm drunk, Alan."

Alan stood, uncaring of several glances observing his own unsteady stance. He fumbled with De-Ann's cape before placing the soft white velvet over her shoulders.

De-Ann wavered but forced herself to walk out of the room slowly, feeling curiously detached from her surroundings. Determined her queasy stomach would not revolt, she clasped her evening bag, head bowed in concentration. She walked unevenly to the elevators, Alan's hand gripping her arm firmly.

Holding on to each other, they descended to the lower floor, the sudden stop causing De-Ann's stomach to turn. She leaned into Alan as they walked through the entrance doorway. The brisk air blowing in from the bay momentarily refreshed them as they waited for Alan's car to be brought to the entrance.

Assisted into the front seat of Alan's bright red Corvette by the valet, De-Ann smiled her thanks before leaning her head gratefully against the seat back. A shiver shook her slender figure at the early-morning dampness. It was a startling contrast from the heated dining room.

Seated behind the wheel, Alan was unaware he was being watched. With a squeal of tires he pulled carelessly from the parking area.

Sudden warmth from the heater was too much for De Ann. She slumped dejectedly, stomach clenching, eyes closed tight, as she tried unsuccessfully to keep the black depths of faintness from overtaking her reeling mind.

Derek Howell motioned to a waiting cab driver, then hurriedly placed his irate blond companion in the rear seat. He thrust a wad of bills in the driver's hand before striding, without a backward look, to his waiting car. Within moments he was screeching from the parking lot in pursuit of Alan's Corvette, his white Ferrari traveling rapidly down the near-vacant streets.

Overtaking the weaving automobile, Derek pulled alongside. He eased closer, his horn blaring, until Alan was forced to pull to the curb and stop.

Sullen over Derek's interference, Alan rolled the window down as the older man strode back to him. His eyes refused to meet Derek's arrogant gaze, hands trembling on the wheel with sulky cowardice.

Derek opened the car door, his mood black, anger turning his eyes hard and remote. Pulling Alan roughly from the seat, he demanded furiously, "What the hell are you trying to do, Anderson? You're too drunk to drive, you young fool. You can break your own neck but damned if I'm going to let you kill your date!"

Derek motioned a passing taxi to a halt, then thrust

21

Alan impatiently into the backseat. Again handing the driver a wad of bills, he curtly gave him his passenger's home address.

"Pick up your car in the morning, Anderson," Derek added as a final order, disgust filling his body at Alan's meek submission.

As he strode to the passenger door of the Corvette, Derek contemplated the woman. Out cold from her unaccustomed drinking, she had curled into the corner of the seat, peacefully unaware of what was transpiring.

Derek opened the door, bitterly cursing under his breath. He lifted her slight body easily with his powerful arms and carried her to his Ferrari, where he placed her gently on the soft leather seat and closed the door.

He returned to the Corvette to roll up the window and lock it securely after checking to see it was safely parked on the steep sloping street.

De-Ann never wakened as Derek eased his car over the curving streets, carefully maneuvering up and down the hills to his home overlooking San Francisco Bay. He pulled to a smooth stop in the broad circular drive, frowning as De-Ann murmured incoherently.

Exasperated by her choice of partner, he gathered her into his arms, shuddering as she unconsciously burrowed into his chest. Heady perfume filled his nostrils, its scent and the feel of her limp body affecting him like an unexpected kick in the abdomen.

One elegantly shod heel kicked the front door shut before he ascended the wide curved stairway to the north wing containing his private suite of rooms. With surprising tenderness he laid her on his king-size bed. In the dim light from his nightstand lamp Derek looked broodingly at the lovely young woman enveloped in a long velvet cape. Her innocent face belied the words he overheard when she agreed to spend the night with his attorney's son.

Derek leaned down, his hands deft as he slipped an evening sandal from each small foot. He reached for the zipper on the side of her dress. His large hands trembled at their first contact with the satiny smoothness of ivory skin. Hot blood coursed wildly through his veins. She was the most desirable woman he had ever seen. From the first moment his gaze locked with the wondrous jade-green depths of her stormy eyes, he intended to have her. He vowed Alan would never make love to her again, agreeing she would be a dynamite bedmate for any man.

To tame her fiery temper and quell her defiant personality would add excitement to their future relationship. Confident in his experience with women, Derek never doubted his ability to please the tempestuous beauty sleeping on his bed.

23

CHAPTER TWO

Wakened by the feel of an unfamiliar mattress plus the absence of noise from early-morning commuter traffic, De-Ann moaned from pain. Her head throbbed, her mouth felt dry, her throat constricting as she swallowed with discomfort. Eyes clenched shut, she longed for total oblivion. Forcing her lethargic body to respond, she sat up and with a feeling of hazy disbelief looked around.

Suddenly aware of her nakedness, she clutched the dark gray satin sheet to her naked breasts, as her glance took in the strangeness of the elegantly furnished room. In her distress she tried desperately to remember her evening with Alan, but she shuddered, a tight knot in her stomach, when her memory of the intervening hours went blank. Bending her head, she groaned softly, her hair a silken mane of tumbled curls, falling well past her shoulder blades.

The faint buzzing of an electric razor in use entered her consciousness as she raised her eyes to survey the room. Awed by the sumptuous masculine decor with sleek modern furnishings, black wall-to-wall carpeting, and stark white walls, her heart beat fearfully. She hadn't expected Alan's room to be so potently masculine.

The razor's hum stopped, replaced by the sound of running water. De-Ann looked around frantically for some sign of her clothing, afraid to move for fear of being caught nude out of bed. Paralyzed, she waited for Alan to appear, hopeful for an explanation of her inexcusable behavior.

"Oh, no," she murmured, panic-stricken when she caught sight of the indented pillow next to hers. Tears of shame brimmed in her eyes as her mind reeled with remorse at the thought that she had slept with Alan.

Her face raised as the sound of running water stopped. She sat wide-eyed, motionless and frightened, in the crumpled bed, desperately trying to remember beyond the moment she stepped into Alan's car.

The door opened abruptly. Still damp from the shower, Derek paused, drops of moisture glistening on his unruly hair. With roguish eyes he stared boldly at his guest, his sensual lips raised in a teasing half smile. Amused by her shocked expression, he waited for the certain outburst.

De-Ann's eyes widened, dark jade pools of shock in her pale face, as she stared openmouthed.

"You! Oh, my God, I slept with . . . you," she cried out before lowering her face to her hands, eyes clenched shut. Jolted to the depth of her being by the sight of Derek's near-naked torso, she tried to hide her feeling of trauma.

Intrigued by her reaction, Derek walked to the bed. Briefly one well-groomed hand touched her shoulder as his deep voice penetrated her profound thoughts.

"Why so upset? You were planning to sleep with that idiot Alan. I daresay I'm better in bed than he'll ever be. At least I've never had any complaints about my abilities as a lover," he added without conceit. "Nor do I ever get too drunk to drive my date home."

25

De-Ann moaned, refusing to glance upward. Drops clung to her lowered lashes in a vain attempt to hold back tears of mortification. She kept her eyes tightly closed, afraid Derek had removed the short towel wrapped around his lean hips.

She stiffened as the bed gave to his weight and he sat beside her. The spread tightened across her thighs as he leaned forward, his clean male scent filling her nostrils. Her slender shoulders quivered as she tried to force her foggy mind to respond with a quick solution to the dilemma caused by his proximity.

Derek reached forward. One long tanned finger raised her chin; his narrowed eyes scrutinized her tear-filled eyes. Her thick spiky lashes were damp as they fluttered to conceal the fear of what she had done, her eyes deep misty pools of self-disgust.

"Look at me, my auburn-haired beauty," Derek commanded.

De-Ann shook her head, refusing to meet his piercing blue eyes, eyes that looked as if they could see into her soul.

"Open your eyes, lovely one," he reiterated his command. Letting his finger trail leisurely over her quivering lower lip, he enjoyed its soft silkiness beneath his fingertip. He leaned forward, his lips gently seeking her sensitive earlobe. He nibbled, seducing her with his expertise. She sat motionless, shaken by his touch. His voice thickened, sounding loud in the quiet room. "You're all soft and warm . . and receptive."

De-Ann's lashes flickered, and she drew her head back to meet his eyes. Their glances locked until she was forced to look away from the compelling intimacy. She clutched frantically at the slipping sheet, covering the heaving agitation of her firm breasts.

A smile tugged at his lips, amusement glittering in his

eyes, when she pulled away. "My touch isn't that bad, is it? After all, we did sleep together."

His spell over her senses was broken as she cried out in disbelief. "But I couldn't have. I've never . . . been with a . . . man . . . before."

His expression changed and his voice grew sardonic. "I figured you'd be more honest than to try that old ploy. Are you forgetting I was the one who watched you laying all over Alan last night? I saw you encourage his caresses and heard you agree to sleep with him."

"No!" she cried, the sound of her voice painfully unfamiliar. His nearness caused her to shiver, and she shook her head from side to side to dispute his words, her eyes pleading for him to believe her. "I—I didn't."

Derek shrugged nonchalantly, his expression enigmatic. "Don't worry about it." His hand slid to cup her bare shoulder briefly while his eyes lingered on her parted lips.

His shaving lotion made her senses whirl, the scent a fresh woodsy odor. The bronzed muscles of his broad shoulders rippled as he removed his hand to spread it next to her thigh. A springy mat of dark hair clung to his powerful, sculpted pectoral muscles. Her eyes followed it down his flat abdomen as it tapered to his navel, exposed above the white shag towel still wound tightly around his lean masculine hips. His legs were long and taut, the skin deeply tanned beneath the scattering of dark hair covering their manly shape.

Emotion churned between the two as De-Ann lifted her gaze reluctantly from his entrancing nudity. Her heart beat wildly as she sensed that he was going to place his sensual mouth over hers. Her lips parted involuntarily, even white teeth a faint line against her velvety mouth as she waited expectantly.

But she came to her senses abruptly and cried out, "No . . . no, don't!" She clung with desperation to the satin top sheet, the only covering to her trembling nakedness, as she scooted to the other side of the bed.

Derek sat back, laughing with a deep throaty sensuality. His eyes darkened with awareness, the deep blue irises lingering on the mature fullness of her heaving breasts.

"Don't be so skittish. I was only going to answer the invitation on your parted lips. Soft red lips that beseeched me to taste them."

"No . . . no, I wasn't," she whispered poignantly before changing the subject abruptly. "How did I get undressed?" Afraid, she waited, though she knew the answer only too well.

"I undressed you," he explained, amused by her sudden touch of color. "Did you think I would let my manservants enjoy the beauty of your unblemished, ivory-tinted skin? I found it extremely pleasant to remove each wispy article concealing the perfection of your delectable feminine curves. Your naked body is a gorgeous sight, a vision I'll not easily forget."

Sobbing angrily, she glared at him, appalled by the mischievous glint in his eyes. "How could you be so—so—uncouth? Why didn't you at least leave on my underwear or put me in a pair of your pajamas?"

"My sweet . . . not-so-innocent . . . consort, I wouldn't have a pair of those things in my house. Too restricting." Derek stood and strode purposefully around the wide bed. "Kiss me once, then I'll leave you to dress for work. Despite our enjoyable night—er—together, I'm too busy to play during the day."

"Kiss you? Why, you—you monstrous brute . . . I hate you!" De-Ann flashed out, watching him warily. Her temper returned; her eyes sparked with anger. Ready to let fire verbally if he took another step forward, she threatened, "If you come one inch closer, you'll be sorry. I'll—I'll call your servants!"

28

Derek threw his head back, deep laughter resounding in the room. "Call all you like. This portion of the house is soundproof, and they only come here when I ring."

Uncaring of De-Ann's threats, Derek lowered himself to the bed, his overpowering arrogance hypnotizing her. His mouth hovered above hers for one long torturous moment. Both hands clasping her shoulders dwarfed their slenderness while the warmth of his breath fanned her face.

De-Ann shut her eyes, waiting for a ruthless plundering by his firm mouth. She heard a soft pleading whimper, unaware at first it was coming from deep within her throat. She felt his thumbs move seductively over her shoulders, slowly, as if savoring the feel of their smooth texture.

Expecting a harsh, brutal kiss, De-Ann remained speechless when Derek placed a featherlight touch to her closed eyelids, pale cheekbones, and the corner of her mouth. She was shocked by her unusual submission but she anticipated his next move.

Derek released her to stand up. Exasperated, he exhaled, then berated her sardonically. "Damn it, woman, you're acting like a frightened virgin with your eyes clenched shut and trembling hands holding the sheet over your beautiful breasts. Were you expecting ravishment by the devil?"

De-Ann flushed at Derek's choice of words, having the fleeting sensation she had already been ravished. Watching him walk away, she sighed with relief before blurting out petulantly: "Why didn't you let me sleep in a guest room?"

Derek stopped, looking at her over his shoulder, his deep voice thick and harsh. "Don't credit me with virtues I don't have. I would never pass up the unexpected pleasure of holding a naked nubile body in my arms. Especially one offered so pleasantly."

"My Lord, no. I couldn't have. Not with you. I don't even know you," De-Ann cried out in confusion, her thoughts in a turmoil.

"Last night we didn't. This morning we know each other rather intimately, I'd say." His bantering changed abruptly, his voice warning her seriously. "Stay there while I dress. Despite sleeping together, I know nothing about you. Don't move!" His sharp command was that of a man used to authority and explicit obedience. When he left the room without a backward glance, it was obvious he expected her to remain in his bed.

Relief at Derek's departure gave her the sudden energy she needed. Without a second's hesitation De-Ann scrambled from the bed, his oversize sheet held around her body as she searched through the room for her clothes.

With a sigh of satisfaction she found her dress and cape neatly folded, laying on the cushion of a chair. Not bothering even to hunt for her underwear or shoes, she pulled the dress over her head, fingers fumbling with nervousness on the side zipper. Afraid he would reappear, she jerked the cape around her shoulders and ran from the room. She rushed down the long hall to the stairway, her bare feet silent on the plush carpeting, and fled down the stairs. As she opened the wide double doors her heart beat frantically, expecting Derek's firm grip to stop her impetuous flight.

Outside she ran as if her life depended on it, crying out when she spotted a delivery truck. She stopped the driver and pleaded with him to drive her to the nearest taxi stand.

Her tear-stained face softened his heart as he let her in. Dropping her several blocks from his route, he watched her get into a parked cab. The effusive thank-you lingered as he drove away, her appearance a welcome change in his mundane job.

De-Ann glared at the young taxi driver's knowing expression when she asked him to drive her to her apartment across town. He cynically followed her upstairs and waited outside her open front door to be sure he didn't get cheated of his fare.

De-Ann rifled through her dresser, hunting for money. She thrust the fare into his hand, plus a generous tip despite her annoyance at his forward manner.

The young driver tipped his hat, then swaggered back to his cab, eager to tell his buddies about the gorgeous dish he delivered from the exclusive section of private mansions to apartment row. He concluded she was returning from a wild all-night party; her bare feet and disarray made him envious of the man who had been her partner. Least he could have done was give her taxi fare home, he thought. Pulling from the curb, he shrugged complacently, agreeing he surely met all kinds in his job.

De-Ann locked her front door firmly, hating the knowing look of the cocky young driver. Walking into her bedroom, she tore the elegant evening dress roughly from her body. She entered the small neat bathroom and stepped into the shower. The water was icy cold, a shock to her heated body. It soothed her tormented mind, helping ease her raging headache. After scrubbing furiously, she lathered her hair with scented shampoo before turning slowly around to let the sharp spray purge her body of her lingering hangover.

Cleansed, free of makeup and the feel of Derek's tantalizing touch, she went to her dresser and plugged in the blow dryer. She let the warm air dry the damp strands until they lay in thick smooth waves around her shoulders.

De-Ann phoned her secretary to explain she would be delayed for another hour. She dressed carefully, pulling on

31

a flared gray-and-black-plaid skirt over a form-fitting black body shirt. Slipping her feet into knee-high black boots, she fastened a narrow belt around her waist, then sat down to apply her makeup with a deft, practiced hand.

She refused to think of her disastrous evening. She was not yet willing to examine the consequences of her inexcusable behavior and excessive drinking, so she drove it to the back of her mind as she descended the steep stairs to the small street-level garage. De-Ann, though of average height, had long legs that gave her a look of elegance and sophistication. Her graceful carriage and striking flare for color and design made people assume on first acquaintance that she was either an actress or a dancer.

In her gleaming bronze Mazda RX-7 she drove to work, but her mind was on Derek, wondering why she had acted so contrarily to her normal personality. Without his presence it seemed impossible that she, a mature, responsible, outspoken adult, had actually submitted to a stranger's mischievous sexual overtures. Any other man would have been put in place with a few well-chosen words. She excused her actions, assuming her brain had been dulled by too much alcohol.

She stopped in front of a small shop in the central area of town, pleased to find a vacant parking place. Her name on the window caused a triumphant smile to raise her lips when she realized her success had been achieved solely through her talent, constant vigor, and perseverance.

Pushing open the glass door of De-Ann's, she entered the vibrantly colored shop. A profusion of green plants, two high-back velour chairs, one on each side of a gilt end table, her own hand-loomed rug of thick yarn in an abstract pattern, and eye-catching wall decorations made it appear custom-decorated. The long glass-covered counter displayed an assortment of her work; a large leather portfolio held more examples of her unique talent.

Smiling at her young secretary sitting behind the counter surreptitiously reading a lurid covered paperback, De-Ann greeted her.

"Good morning, Julie."

"Hi, there, De-Ann," she answered, pushing her book into the bottom drawer of her desk before handing over the morning mail.

De-Ann scanned the mail, thumbing carelessly through the usual assortment of bills before asking her secretary, "Did Charles Percy phone?"

"Not yet."

"Good. I've been thinking about his project and I need a little more time to decide if I can spare him the time."

A well-trained calligrapher with a natural flair for the dramatic, De-Ann had a unique talent that was in constant demand. Once in her back office she perched on the corner of her desk in the larger, well-lighted room. Taking two aspirin and sipping a cup of hot black coffee, she contemplated her day's work.

Her large work desk with its slanted top beneath a bright nonglare light contained sheets of expensive parchment paper. The hand-lettered awards for several city employees who were nearing retirement were almost finished. Each one was a work of art, lettered in her elegant professional form and suitable for framing.

De-Ann's beautiful penmanship and impeccable style of exacting lettering were as elaborate and precise as any of the old masters. Her matchless talent was pursued by the discriminating in a field that was limited to few and quickly becoming a lost art form.

Returning to the front, she watched the youthful face of her plump, pleasant-natured secretary. De-Ann frowned for a brief moment, thinking Julie too immature to have a husband and two tiny children at not yet twenty-one years old.

33

Feeling unsettled and years older, De-Ann asked Julie to get her a 2½ mm Brause nib to do the menu of a new Mongolian barbecue restaurant. "I think I'll finish the awards by one or two o'clock, then I might as well start on the menu. With the way prices keep rising I'll probably need to change it each week." She asked with interest about her secretary's children and listened attentively as Julie extolled their virtues, before returning to her back office.

Propped on a high stool, her heels clinging to the metal bracing, she was soon immersed in the fine detail of lettering in ornate Roman Gothic print each employee's name on gilded parchment.

The balance of the morning passed swiftly, time having no meaning, as De-Ann concentrated on her exacting work. Glancing up, she was surprised to see Julie standing beside her. De-Ann straightened her tight back, wiggling her shoulders to ease their stiffness. "Time for lunch already?" she asked, smiling.

"Yes. Do you want me to bring you anything back?" Her secretary's plain face was bright and complacent as she waited.

"Hmmm . . . check the refrigerator for me. If there's no yogurt, bring me a cup of boysenberry, please."

De-Ann reached for some money on the cabinet next to her and handed Julie a dollar bill. "Buy me the kind with the fruit on the bottom. I prefer it. And thanks, Julie."

Turning back to her work, she barely listened as the outer doorbells jingled when her secretary left. Intent on her printing, she was annoyed when the phone rang.

She laid her pen staff down and capped the black ink before lifting the receiver. "De-Ann's."

"Hi, De-Ann. Did you get home okay?"

Recognizing Alan's embarrassed voice, De-Ann

frowned, furious at him for letting her get into such a predicament.

"Fat lot you care, Alan!" she hissed, her temper rising as she thought of what had happened during the early-morning hours.

"I apologize. Apparently you're all right though and nothing unusual happened. Guess I drank too much."

"You not only drink too much, you talk too much." Thinking of her traumatic night and his careless assumption that nothing had happened, De-Ann lit into Alan with a fury that matched her auburn hair and ended with, "Don't call me again, Alan. I refuse to go out with any man so irresponsible that he can't even see his date gets home safely."

"Derek didn't do anything to you, did he?" he asked fearfully.

"Of course not," she lied easily. "I was home in bed within ten minutes of the time he picked me up."

"Good. I told you he's quite a womanizer and warned you that if you interested him he would have you in his bed within hours of your first meeting."

More like minutes, she thought, hanging up the phone and deliberately interrupting his petulant apologetic words. Too angry to talk, she stomped to her work desk and climbed onto the stool. Her hands trembling, she took too much ink on her pen nib and blurred the first letter, ruining a sheet of parchment.

De-Ann set the pen down, forcing herself to calm down. She knew she couldn't work while still ired: Alan hadn't bothered to inquire about her safety till noon.

Grumbling about men, she paced the back office and was reading over her mail for the second time when the doorbell jingled and Julie burst in carrying two sacks.

"Here's your yogurt, De-Ann." Julie handed her boss the small bag and the change and returned to her own desk. Munching on potato chips, a deli submarine sandwich, and a package of cupcakes, and drinking a can of cold soda pop while reading a romantic novel, she dreamed of being as glamorous and shapely as her elegant boss.

Pushing the thought of Alan aside, De-Ann shut her eyes. Derek Howell's image immediately filled her mind. His overpowering maleness was not easy to forget. She doubted if she would ever get over the shock of seeing his broad frame outlined in his bathroom door. The perfection of his almost naked body was etched on her mind as clearly as her best calligraphy, each detail as emphatic and lucid as her own penmanship.

Lord, she thought, *he's such a perfect male animal.* His sun-bronzed body had dwarfed the massive room and everything in it as he stood braced in a skimpy towel staring at her with teasing eyes. His rock-hard muscles appeared smooth as molten steel, graceful and elegant despite their masculine sinewy lines. His flat stomach and lean hips supported by straight legs, taut thighs, and well-defined calves were perfectly proportioned for his brawny torso.

Rubbing her forehead, De-Ann reluctantly admitted she had wanted to run her sensitive fingertips over every inch of Derek's striking body. She had felt a longing to touch him as if he were a statue and she was the artist who had created him.

She was disappointed he had not possessed her mouth: she could imagine the sparks that would ignite when his firm, sensual lips touched hers. She ached to feel the devastation his practiced caresses could arouse.

Kissing was not a novelty to De-Ann. Dating frequently from the age of fifteen, she had started with boys eager to learn, progressing to men eager to teach. But she had often been disappointed and had never been moved beyond the placid enjoyment of knowing she was a desirable woman.

De-Ann thought of Derek's arrogant, commanding personality, realizing instinctively he would not be satisfied with a lukewarm response like she had given in the past. He would demand and pursue until his woman was a quivering mass of femininity eager to give until there was nothing left, then begging to receive all he had to offer in return.

Disgusted with recurring thoughts of Derek Howell tormenting her when she had tasks to complete, De-Ann propped her hip against the high work stool before opening the carton of yogurt. With each tasty mouthful of tart creamy yogurt she felt more confident that she was over her irritation with Alan's juvenile behavior and that Derek was only a bad memory.

Finished, she threw the empty carton in the wastebasket, washed her hands, applied fresh lipstick, and was soon immersed in her exacting penmanship.

She checked her watch after finishing the last award, breathing a sigh of relief. Within the hour Julie would be leaving and she could lock the doors. Her time alone in the evening, with the shop secure and shades drawn, was always welcome. Assured of no interruptions, she accomplished her most important work.

De-Ann called her secretary, asking, "Julie, check with the restaurant owner before I start his menu. He liked Uncial letters, but I think Far Eastern would be more appropriate."

"Sure, De-Ann," Julie answered pleasantly. As she reached for the phone to dial, it rang. "De-Ann's. Yes, Mr. Anderson, she's right here." Holding her hand over the mouthpiece, Julie called her boss. "Alan's on the phone, De-Ann."

De-Ann picked up the phone, storming furiously at him

37

for the second time that day. "I thought I told you not to call me again, Alan!"

"You did . . . but you also told me that Derek Howell took you home within ten minutes of putting me in a taxi."

"Well, what about it?" she demanded crossly.

"You lied, my sweets. He just left the house. He wanted your home address. Seems he forgot to get it when you woke this morning. He also casually mentioned that he had a bra, garter belt, panties, nylon hose, and sandals that belong to you."

"Why, that dirty . . .!" Embarrassed to be caught lying and subject to suspicions she knew were going through Alan's mind, she spluttered with barely controlled anger. "That dirty, ruthless monster. I could kill him for this."

"A little late for that, isn't it? You should have told him how you felt instead of climbing into his bed. Why the hell did you do it, De-Ann?"

"I didn't 'do it' as you think, Alan. I passed out and Derek let me stay at his house for the night. That's all that happened."

"That's not what he said. He thanked me for bringing you to the restaurant and drinking so much that he felt it necessary to put me in a taxi. He also claimed you were the most beautiful, receptive woman he had ever held in his arms. Furthermore he told me to get any ideas out of my head about dating you anymore as he staked his claim last night and you are now his private property!"

"He what? That dirty swine! I absolutely loathe the man. Don't believe a word of it, Alan. I don't know what he's up to, but when I find out, he'll wish he never saw me."

Her hands shook with fury; her eyes glittered jade-green sparks of temper. She was so angry, she was speechless. Listening to Alan's pleading voice as he complained petulantly, she stood, hand on hip, one foot tapping restlessly.

"For six months I couldn't get to first base with you, and that bastard scored the first night. Damn it, De-Ann, why the hell did you let him have you?"

"I didn't!"

"I don't believe you. Derek was too . . . convincing."

"Don't believe me, then, Alan. I don't give a damn," De-Ann blurted out recklessly. Her voice was so loud, she didn't hear the front doorbell jingle, nor, standing with her back to the front office, did she see the tall dark man enter her shop.

"What do you want me to say? That I spent the night stark naked in Derek's king-size bed between rumpled gray satin sheets? That I woke feeling better than I've ever felt in my life after hours and hours of making mad, passionate love together and I think he is the most handsome, virile, dynamic man I have ever met? That I fell wildly in love with him and hope he makes love to me every night for the rest of my life?

"Well, Alan Anderson, if that's what you want to believe, then believe it. I don't give a damn about you or any other man in the entire world!"

De-Ann slammed down the receiver, her body trembling with anger. Her head pounded with a raging headache for the second time that day. Burying her face in her hands, she sobbed brokenly, unchecked tears streaming down her pale cheeks.

She forgot her secretary, wishing she could slip into oblivion until her world that had been so peaceful until that morning righted itself and the dreadful nightmare she was living came to an end.

39

CHAPTER THREE

Julie's startled eyes linked with Derek's as he entered De-Ann's shop. She recognized his dark good looks immediately. She was painfully aware of the damaging implication of the one-sided conversation he overheard with intense interest, but unsure what to do, she stared open-mouthed.

Holding a finger to his lips to silence her, Derek listened to the end of De-Ann's boisterous tirade. He whispered to Julie to get her purse and go home. She obeyed without hesitation, assured by his confident manner that her employer would be all right.

As Julie scurried out the door with a last backward glance at De-Ann, Derek smiled kindly. "She'll be fine now. Believe me, please."

He locked the door before walking boldly into the back room. His expression was unreadable as he scanned the dejected appearance of De-Ann's trembling figure. Oblivious of Derek's entrance, she sobbed loudly, her plaintive cries resounding through her office. Obviously moved, he walked stealthily behind her and gathered her into his arms.

She was startled by his touch but knew instantly who held her. Wrenching free of his loose hold, she turned on him with the fury of a woman who had reached the end of her patience. Her small hands struck futilely at his chest as she tried to explain the reason for her fury between convulsive sobs.

He thought her beautiful in her anger, lustrous auburn hair tumbling about her pale face, darkened eyes shimmering with tears. Barely feeling her hands battering his chest, he let her vent her anger before gathering her into the security of his strong and comforting hold.

Holding both her hands easily in his large palm, Derek murmured soothing words as she cried out poignantly.

"I hate you! I—I absolutely loathe you."

"I know, sweetheart. I know. Get it all out of your system, then we'll talk." Derek buried his face in the silky-soft strands of her gleaming hair, inhaling its heady scent as she continued to berate him. After her racking sobs subsided, he raised her chin from his chest and let his eyes linger on the loveliness of her face.

"Why did you lie to Alan about me?" she asked him.

"I didn't."

"Yes, you did! He thinks we made love all night long."

"*I* didn't tell him that. You did."

Forgetting to fight Derek for a moment, De-Ann stared, feeling a hot flush color her cheeks at the knowledge he had overheard her conversation with Alan.

"You heard?"

"Yes. Every single word." Derek slid his hands up and down De-Ann's spine in a soothing gesture while she contemplated his reaction to her blatant declarations to Alan.

"Oh, Lord. I could die of embarrassment."

"Why? Someday it will all be true. Every single word."

41

She wrenched free from his clasp and stood glaring arrogantly at him, hands on hips. "You'll be the last man I will ever go to bed with!"

"I know. That is what I intended from the moment I first saw you."

"That isn't what I meant and you know it . . . you—you swine!"

"Hush!" A thread of steel ran through his voice in warning. "I don't want to hear any more lies from you."

Not heeding Derek's firm admonition, De-Ann continued. "They aren't lies. You *are* a swine. A ruthless man who has permanently ruined my relationship with Alan."

"I know and that was my intention. He's not for you and you know it. Everything I told him was the truth."

"How could it be?" she blurted out, firm breasts rising and falling with each breath. "He said you told him I was your property."

"You are," Derek answered matter-of-factly.

Infuriated by his assured manner and deep, confident voice, De-Ann reached toward her work table. She picked up a bottle of black ink and threw it at him in a surge of uncontrolled wrath.

Derek ducked easily, and the bottle struck a wooden cabinet behind him, breaking and splattering ink on the carpet. He frowned as his manner changed from one of quiet consideration to that of a man used to being obeyed.

"Quit it!" His voice cut through the room like a knife.

But De-Ann was too incensed. She grabbed another bottle and brought her arm back to hurl it.

"Drop it!" he ordered. Quick and agile, Derek moved forward, catching her wrist and squeezing until she released the bottle. As he pulled her ruthlessly against his granite-hard chest, the bottle fell to the carpeted floor and rolled, unbroken, under her desk.

Not at all intimidated, De-Ann kicked out, her boot toe

making painful contact with his shin. Her continued defiance surprised him, causing his temper to explode. His mouth took hers in a savage kiss as he lifted her off her feet to meet his lips. Her lips were parted with sudden swiftness in a kiss meant to punish and control. One hand gripped her nape mercilessly, the other spread across her stiff back. Penetrating the depths of her mouth, his tongue probed, demanding her total submission.

Enraged, De-Ann refused to give in and squirmed helplessly.

Derek released her mouth and commanded, his breath fanning her face, "Quit fighting me. You can't win and you'll only get hurt!"

Amazed by her refusal to surrender to his greater strength, he lowered his head the slight distance separating their faces.

De-Ann attempted to sink her teeth into Derek's lower lip, vainly trying to draw blood. But Derek was waiting for her next rebellious act and his reflexes were quick. His hands cupped her face with strong broad palms before he possessed her mouth in a savage kiss.

Faint with shock from the first moment his lips had touched hers, she fought valiantly to restrain her desire to respond. Her tempestuous unawakened sensuality rose to the surface, seeking relief in expression.

She moaned as the assault on her mouth continued. Her body melded involuntarily to his. The desire to fight him left in a blazing surge of unbearable ecstasy aroused by his mastery.

Her hands slid to his neck, threaded through the thick raven-black hair, each fingertip sensitive to the feel of the unruly waves. Her lips softened, mouth parting to respond to his probing tongue, the intimacy of his stimulating touch inciting her latent passions. Her breasts tautened, the nipples firm peaks the instant she felt one hand leave her face to clasp her nape, the other to cup a swelling curve.

With deliberate purpose he rubbed the throbbing nipple until she squirmed to elude the shocking cravings that swept all protest temporarily aside. His touch searing her skin, she reeled, the room beginning to spin as his mouth left her swollen lips to clamp seductively on the side of her neck.

She felt blood coursing through her veins. His kiss was all she had thought it could be and more. Her heart hammered with unbridled excitement knowing he could stir her like no other man had. She wrapped her arms around his lean hips, clinging to his body until her quivering limbs could not carry her from the overpowering strength of his arms.

Pleased at her sudden yielding, Derek slipped his hand inside the low neckline of her blouse. He ached to feel the satiny texture of her naked skin. As his fingers stroked the delectable fullness of her breast, he could feel the buildup of her fiery temper. God, what a woman, he thought. She was the most exciting female in the world. The taste of her sweet mouth would haunt his nights until she spent them in his arms.

De-Ann pulled from Derek's intimate touch, slapping his wrist furiously as her independence surged back. "Damn you, Derek . . . quit that! I've never allowed a man to touch me there before and I don't intend to start with a . . . stranger."

"I did last night."

"Oh, God, no. You didn't, did you?" she flared back.

"Yes. I told you I laid no claim to virtue around a beautiful woman who racked my body with desire. I placed a fleeting caress on the tip of each breast with my hands . . . and mouth."

"I can't believe it. What else did you do?" she moaned.

"I looked at you until I felt as if I knew your body as well as my own."

"Oh, no . . . you're sick!" she cried out, shaking her head in shame as she imagined him viewing her naked body without restraint. "No man has ever seen me unclothed before."

"I have. Every tantalizing curve. I'm ruthless when I see something I want, and, my dear beautiful bundle of fire and passion, I want and intend to have you—every inch of you!"

"Never! Get out of my shop! Get out of my life!" De-Ann rushed to her desk. She grabbed the receiver, preparing to dial. "I'm going to call the police and have you arrested for assault."

Derek leaned his hip casually against her desk, telling her calmly, "Go ahead."

Wary at his unexpected acceptance of her threat, she hesitated, raising her eyes to stare at his enigmatic face. His eyes held hers, hypnotizing her and making her unable to stand up to his dominant personality. Her lashes fluttered, and with a deep sigh she turned her back after slowly replacing the receiver.

"That's better. Are you ready now to listen to me without fighting my every word?" He swung his leg nonchalantly back and forth, his muscular thighs outlined by the fit of smooth gray slacks. He watched her, amused by the indecision raging through her mind, satisfied to wait quietly for her answer.

Her chin angled proudly, jade eyes flashing as she nodded in agreement, refusing to voice her consent.

"Say it!"

"What?"

"That you won't fight me anymore today."

A brief glimmer of temper flared before she acquiesced.

"Okay. I'm too weary and confused by the last few hours to want to fight anyone now."

"Good. Now show me around your shop and tell me what you do. Are you responsible for all the beautiful calligraphy I saw on your counter when I entered?"

De-Ann announced proudly that it indeed was all her work. She was surprised, though, by Derek's show of interest and the sincere look in his eyes.

"You are not only beautiful, you're exceedingly talented in a unique field. Where did you train?"

De-Ann's animosity fled as she told him about her flair for design since childhood and her interest in calligraphy from her first introduction in fairy tale stories. She found herself relaxing in his company for the first time. Without questioning her reasons, she opened up to him, explaining about her Bachelor of Arts degree and long years establishing her shop until it was now a highly profitable but time-consuming occupation.

"I could use your talents in many of my business interests. Do you do sketches as well as calligraphy?"

"Yes. Let me show you my portfolio. I have numerous copies of pen-and-ink drawings that I incorporated with my penmanship. I must warn you that I'm very expensive," she added over her shoulder as she walked into the front office. She picked up the large leather folder to show him an example of her art work.

"I like expensive things if the quality is there." His eyes lingering on her slender back and the curve of her rounded hips, he laughed suggestively, his words having a double meaning.

Derek thumbed carefully through her portfolio. He was amazed by the graceful beauty of her work. The fine lines were perfect to the most intimate detail. There were sketches of wildflowers for thank-you notes, herbs and spices for cookbooks, and brides and grooms for wedding announcements. Detailed outlines of houses, shopping centers, and real estate developments would please the most exacting architect.

Impressed to the point of being stunned, Derek looked at De-Ann with narrowed eyes. "These are exquisite. What do you net a year?"

She told him without hesitation and waited for his comment.

"Good, but not good enough. Your overhead here is too high for the location. I could set you up in a better area and supply you with enough work from my companies alone to double your profit the first year."

De-Ann shook her head in disagreement, explaining ruefully, "No, thank you. I've been independent too long to be tempted by your generous offer. I like being my own boss and running everything my own way. I don't think I could tolerate any interference, and you are much too bossy to allow me the freedom I'm used to."

Derek's deep laughter rang through the small front office as he leaned his head back in amusement. "I can see you are going to cause me problems, Ms. Wagner. That's the first time in my life I recall a woman turning down a chance to make money off me."

"Well it's about time one did, then! You are much too arrogant and demanding." De-Ann took her portfolio after Derek finished looking through it, and placed it back on the counter. Turning around, she looked at him thoughtfully. "You'd better leave now, Derek. I have a menu to complete tonight and I'm hours late already. Oh, my gosh, I forgot about poor Julie. Did you scare my secretary away?"

"No, but I did tell her to go home. I preferred to be alone when I first confronted you. Your fury was threatening to explode uncontrollably and I thought I might have to use drastic measures to subdue it." Checking his watch,

47

he asked with concern, "Have you eaten a hot meal to-day?"

"No, I was too upset over last night. I ate boysenberry yogurt at noon, while contemplating how much I hated you."

"No wonder you're so slim," he said, grimacing at the thought of eating yogurt. "Why don't you repair the damage of our altercation and let me take you out to dinner?"

"No, Derek. Thank you anyway but I'm tired and I prefer to finish my work, then go home for a good night's sleep—alone."

"No deal. You're too upset to work tonight. I'll take you to a place I know close by, feed you a high-protein dinner, and escort you home with a chaste good-bye at the door of your apartment."

She agreed, his suggestion suddenly irresistible. Within minutes her makeup was repaired, worktable straightened, and outer door secured, and she was being helped into his gleaming white Ferrari.

Leaning against the soft black leather upholstery, De-Ann laughed. "Did I really ride home—er—to *your* home in this last night?"

"Right in that very seat, cuddling next to me contentedly," Derek teased, before easing into the heavy traffic.

She clenched her handbag nervously, bright spots of color staining her cheeks while her lashes lowered in embarrassment.

"Don't think about it," he reassured her, his mind aware of her humiliation. "I did nothing but hold you. Actually I hadn't intended sleeping with you until you woke up, but you clung to my neck after I undressed you. After that I had no qualms about embracing you until daybreak. The way you felt, pressed against the length of my body, your naked curves soft and warm, while I held

48

you platonically had to be worse than your torment not knowing I did it."

"I still can't believe what happened. I meant it when I told you I had never slept with a man," she told him solemnly. "I'm glad I slept through the whole thing."

De-Ann turned her head, watching him in the flashing lights as they drove through the darkened city. "It embarrasses me to think you've seen me naked. It's so intimate, yet we're strangers," she told him honestly.

"We aren't strangers now. Not after last night. It's a damn good thing you didn't wake before daylight then because I would have taken you, De-Ann." His gaze swept the shadowed outline of her curvaceous figure. "What was it you said to Alan? That you were wildly in love with me and hoped I would make love to you every night for the rest of your life?" His mouth curved mischievously. "I'm no superman but I'd sure give that idea one hell of a try."

"Quit teasing, Derek, or take me home," De-Ann scolded firmly.

Derek reached over with his right hand, clasping her knee briefly. "Okay, beautiful one. I'll be an angel from now on."

"One with a tarnished halo and tattered wings, I imagine." She chuckled, her soft throaty laughter a pleasure to his ears.

"You continue to surprise me, Ms. Wagner. You are a gorgeous creature to look at, delectable to make love to, tempting to fight with, talented to the extreme, sharp with your replies, and you have the ability to make me laugh besides. A perfect companion for the most discriminating man."

"My secretary reads all the gossip about you and she tells me you aren't the most discriminating of men when it comes to women," she shot back, uncertain how to take his personal comments.

Derek gave her a wry glance and smiled before returning his attention to maneuvering on the steep street. "Minx! That was uncalled for. How else could I know when I taste honey if I hadn't sharpened my taste buds on horseradish beforehand?"

"From what I've been told, you have been in the honey pots since you were a young boy!" De-Ann earnestly enjoyed their sharp repartee and was forced to admit that she felt totally relaxed in his company. She watched him covertly as he drove, her pulsebeat increasing as she scanned his strong profile.

The dark sleeves of his silk shirt clung to his wide shoulders and long powerful arms. Remembering his passionate, dominating kisses, she knew she had correctly assumed his body would be steel hard. He had taut muscles sheathed in the velvet covering of his deeply tanned skin. His personality was irresistible: a combination of fiery mastery and surprising tenderness.

Fast succumbing to his innate character, De-Ann smiled. She felt assured she was intelligent enough to keep their relationship as she wished it. After all, her previous male companions had all been easily managed. But she forgot how unsuccessful she had been with Derek thus far.

Derek stopped and turned the Ferrari's wheels in toward the curb on the steep hill. Turning to her, he announced, "We've arrived."

De-Ann glanced at the small, unpretentious, windowed restaurant, its patrons discreetly hidden behind café curtains. FRANÇOIS, printed in neat gold lettering, was on the entrance door.

"François? I've never heard of it before," De-Ann mentioned as Derek assisted her from the low bucket seat.

"You won't ever forget it, I assure you. He's a fine man and unexcelled as a chef." Opening the door, Derek guided her into a bright room holding no more than a dozen tables. She admired the simple decor with plain white tablecloths and unadorned crockery. He entered with confidence, something she was beginning to take for granted.

A slim, dapper man appeared from the kitchen area, welcomed them warmly, then took them to a secluded table in the rear. His brown eyes sparkled with friendliness as he took hold of De-Ann's hands and raised one gallantly to his lips.

"Toutes mes félicitations, Derek, mon ami." Turning back to De-Ann, he shook his head. *"Très belle. Parlez-vous français?"*

De-Ann laughed softly, shaking her head no. Her enchanting eyes filled with laughter at his obvious admiration.

He smiled and switched to English. "Good. I can speak my native tongue now. I was born and bred in California but I feel my customers will leave me if I don't impress them with my high school French."

"Why, you're a fraud! Is your name really François?" she asked, smiling as he seated her himself, brushing Derek's hand aside.

"Frank Smith, would you believe? Somewhere I think I have a French great-grandmother so I'm not a complete charlatan." He turned toward Derek, telling him bluntly, "Keep this one, my friend. She's a beauty, although I don't see you getting all your own way with her. That mane of red hair has to affect her personality. Never met a red-haired woman yet who didn't give her man a hard time."

Winking at De-Ann, Frank added impishly, "Give him hell, honey. He needs it. He has been spoiled by fawning females for years. Now, enjoy your wine while I put the finishing touches on your dinner." With a flourish he left, walking through the swinging doors to the kitchen.

"What's happening now, Derek Howell? Were you expecting to eat dinner here with someone else tonight?" De-Ann quizzed him firmly.

"Of course not."

"But Frank said he was expecting you tonight."

"Of course."

"Why of course?"

"Of course, because I phoned him late this afternoon and told him to have dinner ready for us at eight o'clock." Derek glanced at his watch, smiling smugly. "Right on the dot."

Lowering her voice, De-Ann flared back. "How did you know I would agree to come with you?"

"Intuition."

"Does your intuition tell you I'm getting mad at your high-handed manner?"

"Of course."

"Darn you, Derek. Quit 'of coursing' me all the time."

"Of course!" His lips twitched in an unsuccessful attempt to keep from laughing. Amused, he nonchalantly poured their chilled wine as she fumed with indecision.

"Forget your feminine instinct to show me you are your own boss and enjoy your meal." His cobalt-blue eyes twinkled at her and she relented, her face still flushed with a mutinous expression.

Seldom mad for long, De-Ann laughed quietly before taking a sip of ice water. "If you don't mind, I'll leave the wine for you. After what happened to me this morning, I doubt if I'll ever drink again."

"Nothing happened yet, sweetheart, but soon I can guarantee it will. Very, very soon, my delectable consort."

"Quit it, Derek. No more teasing tonight. I want to enjoy my meal. I suppose I don't even get to order what I want?"

"No. Nor do I. Frank said he'd see we didn't have to

stop for a snack on the way home, and if he says that, dinner will be excellent."

Two hours later, content and replete after a memorable meal, De-Ann lay against the soft cushioned seat of the Ferrari.

"That was scrumptious. I ate every morsel from the tomatoes Gervaise with their cream cheese and chive filling and vinaigrette dressing to the succulent rack of tender spring lamb, *petits pois à la française,* potatoes *boulangére*, and the creamy chocolate mousse."

"Delicious, wasn't it?"

"Yummy. Every single calorie was a delight." Suddenly noticing Derek was driving toward her apartment, De-Ann put her hand on his wrist. "Take me to my shop. I have my car there and I'll drive myself home."

"No."

"Why not?"

"Because that isn't how I operate. I'm either taking you to your apartment, which Alan gave me the address of, or straight back to my home and into my bed. The choice is yours, but make up your mind in a hurry or I'll decide for you. And it damn well won't be in this direction!"

"Lord, you're bossy, Derek. You can't have your own way all the time. Take me to my home then, but that means I'll have to take a bus to work in the morning."

"No, you won't. I intend to leave you taxi fare."

"Oh, no, you won't! You're beginning to make me mad," she retorted impudently. "That would make me feel like a kept woman."

"That also is my intention. Which apartment house is yours?" he questioned, slowing down on her street to check the numbers.

"The cream and rust building between the light blue and navy and the green and white ones."

Derek pulled to the curb in front of the apartment and

stopped the motor. "I enjoy seeing these old homes in San Francisco being restored with a colorful coat of paint. I think this is the most exciting city in the world, with so many houses built side by side undulating over the hills, each with its own personality and interesting occupant."

"They are interesting, aren't they?" Purse in hand, De-Ann reached for the door handle, but was stopped abruptly by Derek's firm voice.

"Sit still!"

De-Ann frowned, glancing over her shoulder. "Now what?"

"I will escort you to your door, check to see your apartment is safe, take my thank-you kiss, and depart."

"Well, three out of four won't be a bad average," she teased mischievously.

"Oh, you mean I don't have to depart?"

"No. I mean you don't get a good-night kiss."

"Apparently you still haven't learned I won't be denied that which I want the most—you!" he warned seriously.

Inhaling the damp foggy air, they walked up the short flight of stairs to her brightly painted front door. De-Ann surrendered the key without protest, standing aside while Derek opened the door.

Switching on the living room light, he glanced around the room. "Just as I imagined. Womanly, exquisitely decorated, impeccably neat, and obviously lacking a man's imprint."

"What did you expect to see? A pipe and large leather slippers next to a satin smoking jacket?" she sassed, setting her purse on a glass-topped end table. She sat down in a velvet chair and clasped her leg behind the knee, holding it out toward him. "Pull."

"What?"

"Pull my boot off. It's easier if I have help and I always go barefoot as soon as I get home."

Derek slipped off first one high-heeled boot then the other. Holding her nylon-clad foot in his broad palm, he was intent on stroking her high arch as he squatted on his heels before her. "According to a television commercial I saw, this is supposed to be the most sensitive part of a woman's body, though I have my doubts."

"You're terrible, Derek," she scolded, jerking her foot from his disturbing touch. "As for me, I find it tickles."

Unfolding his great length to stand in front of her, he admired the shapely curves of her slender form. "Anything else you need help with?"

"Heavens, no. After what happened last night I had better purchase a chastity belt," she teased impudently.

"I have two hobbies—metal work and picking locks!"

"You're hopeless. I never get the last word." She rose, passing him to walk toward her tiny kitchen. "Would you like some coffee?"

"No. Don't make any just for me. I want to look at your apartment." Without a qualm Derek walked into her bedroom, noticing the single bed with brass headboard, bright airy curtains, and matching spread in vivid greens and blues. The abstract pattern blended perfectly with the royal-blue carpeting and kelly-green armchair. Stark white walls were a perfect background for numerous black and white sketches, which he recognized at once as hers.

He looked over the small bathroom with its fluffy towels and countertop covered with perfumes and lotions. He inhaled, aware he was already familiar with her own heady scent.

Finished, he entered the kitchen, watching her fill the percolator with water from the tap. Without her three-inch boot heels she looked even more fragile as he towered in the doorway.

"Save it for breakfast, sweetheart. I'm not thirsty."

"Well, then, what do you want?" she asked without

thinking. Her cheeks flushed a bright rose as she realized how careless her words had been. Waiting for his comment, she eyed him through a fringe of dark lashes. "Well?"

"Well, what?" he taunted, aware she was waiting for him to comment on his blatant need for her.

"Forget it. You never do what I expect anyway."

"Good. That will keep our relationship interesting."

"We have no . . . relationship," she reflected equably after returning the can of coffee back to the overhead cupboard.

"Then what do you call this?" Derek gathered her into his arms, his hands resting possessively on her hips before raising up to cup her face. With his thumbs he forced her chin up to meet his descending mouth.

De-Ann's halfhearted protest died before it left her throat as she found her lips molded beneath his firm mouth in a devastating kiss. She stood on tiptoes, arching to meet his great height, her fingers clinging to his strong neck. Her figure welded to his as he bent her backward against the edge of the tiled counter.

He parted her lips easily, his tongue trailing across the edge of her teeth before entering the tempting moist interior of her mouth.

Her attempt to wrench away was feeble, her senses responding with a deep churning hunger for his touch. Starting in the pit of her stomach, it spread throughout her body. His lips were demanding, their touch possessing her mouth as his body ached to slake its needs in the soft feminine recesses of her body.

His hands left her face to slide down her spine until they reached her hips. As he pressed forward she felt the sharp handle of the cupboard drawer in her back before he shifted her against the hardness of his surging body. The feel of his aroused body was to her heightened nerves a powerful stimulant that left her trembling.

Released from the pressure of his clinging mouth, she felt his lips cross her face to nibble the sensitive skin behind her ear, his face buried in the sweetness of her lustrous hair.

"I've wanted to kiss you like this since the first moment our eyes locked over Alan's head. Your beautiful face expressed such disgust and the beginning of a fine temper."

Reacting to the harsh, unguarded tone of his voice, De-Ann ached to touch him, letting her fingers move from his nape to his heaving chest. She pushed through the shirt buttons, splaying her hand over the springy dark hair that covered his broad chest.

Derek's breath caught as De-Ann's restless fingers explored, her touch more potent than any he previously experienced. His large frame shuddered when she unbuttoned his shirt. Her hands slid to his waist to clasp his bare skin in a tight hug, attempting unsuccessfully to quell her passionate impetuosity.

She burrowed her face against the warmth of his chest, inhaling the clean male scent of his body. His curly hairs tickled her face erotically as she let her lips touch the lean expanse of torso bared by her questing fingers.

Stirred by her first arousal, she responded with an innate sensuousness. She stood on tiptoe to enable her lips to reach the enticing velvety hollow of his lean throat. Oblivious of everything but the need to get closer to Derek, she explored his hard back with restless fingers, pressing her lips fervently on his heated skin.

"God, sweetheart, quit that. I can't stand any more without taking you completely." He felt her back stiffen. He drew back, his palms cupping her shoulders. He scanned her flushed face, aware of her embarrassment and curious about her sexual experience.

"How old are you, De-Ann?" he questioned, his voice deep and husky in the small room.

"Twenty-six." The sound of her name rolling off his tongue was like a continued caress, so utterly masculine, it ran through her body like wildfire.

"Surely you've been kissed and caressed passionately many times before, even if you have still managed to keep yourself intact? There are many—er—technical virgins who permit any lovemaking but the final penetration," he explained bluntly.

"I've been kissed hundreds of times," she answered truthfully, staring into his face. "I have always felt my body was my own and not for anyone else's pleasure unless I wished it so." Spots of color touched each cheek as she continued. "You make me feel like a total innocent, Derek, and according to you I am. I've never been touched intimately or wanted to explore the world of sensuous pleasures."

Her eyes darkening, she explained candidly, "Frankly, tonight with you I wanted to experience everything. I'm telling you this because I know you're aware of my responses. But I am also letting you know I'm aware of my own sexuality and I'll avoid an encounter with you now at all costs!"

"You think so, honey? My God, how naive you are. We are only beginning to love. This is the start, the commencing of a lifetime of learning to satisfy each other's needs. You've awakened me in many ways also. Since you are so candid, I feel it only fair to admit that kissing you was the first time I have felt my control start to slip. You're the first woman I have ever made love to that caused a surge of emotion to penetrate the depth of my soul!"

Derek's hand slid to her chin, caressing it tenderly as

58

he gazed at her wide eyes and fearful expression. "This has been one hell of a day for both of us." He bent to her face and kissed her lips gently, his desire to take her tightly checked. "Go to bed, sweetheart. I'll call you tomorrow."

Derek cast a final look of concern before walking from De-Ann's kitchen. Laying a ten-dollar bill beside her purse for taxi fare, he left as abruptly as he had arrived.

Waves of tiredness rushed over De-Ann as she walked into her living room. Noticing the money, she smiled. Her fingers trembled as they reached up to touch her mouth, which still tingled from Derek's masterful kisses and last tender caress. It seemed impossible that a twenty-four-hour period could affect her life so drastically.

Her thoughts were filled with Derek as she undressed. He was a complex man, assured in his masculinity and bold in his sudden pursuit. She sat before her dresser mirror, brushing her long hair with sure strokes, her shapely body clad in a brief nightgown of kelly-green silk.

"Miss De-Ann Wagner, it's about time you met a man who thrills you from the top of your head to the tips of your toes," she spoke out loud, smiling at her reflection.

She paid no heed to Alan's warning that Derek was deeply cynical toward women. A cynicism that was ingrained since early childhood.

CHAPTER FOUR

De-Ann's step was light the next morning as she arrived at work. Giving the delighted taxi driver a friendly wave, she unlocked the door an hour before her secretary was due to start work.

She checked her ferns to see if they needed water, talking to them excitedly as she sprayed their feathery fronds. "If you really do respond to voices, you should grow today, my beauties. Everything is perfect. The sun is shining radiantly. I feel top-of-the-world and"—checking for dead fronds, her head cocked sideways, soft lips raised in a smile—"I have met the most exciting man in the world, who promised to phone me sometime today." After putting the watering can away, she turned on the lights over her desk.

Humming softly, she prepared her supplies, anxious to start on the menu she had planned to complete the night before. She carefully lined up her work sheet over the properly spaced, lined guidance sheet, then uncapped the ink and reached for her pen.

She proceeded to work, deciding to used closed spacing.

With the staff held firmly in her right hand, nib slanted at the proper angle, she started her stroke. Years of practice and a steady hand made her distinct letters look as if each had been precisely measured before the first serif had been started. Rapidly completing the first page of the complicated menu, she greeted Julie's entrance with a smile.

Julie remembered her boss's temper tantrum and agitation of the previous afternoon and she was uncomfortable until she saw De-Ann's soft expression and glimmering eyes filled with happiness.

"Good morning, Julie. You look lovely today. Isn't this weather glorious?"

"It's super." Julie set her purse on the desk before walking to the back alcove to make their coffee. "Is that a new dress?"

"Yes, another one. Aren't I shameless? I can't pass by anything in green that appeals to me." De-Ann stood up and twirled around. The soft skirt flared around her limbs as she modeled her silk shirtwaister in deep jade green, exactly the color of her eyes.

"Wow, that's really with it," Julie admitted with a touch of envy. Curious at what happened when her boss was alone with Derek Howell, she asked nervously, "Did you and . . . Mr. Howell go out last night?"

"Did we ever! He took me to a fantastic French restaurant for dinner. A little place I had never even heard of. Gourmet cuisine elegantly prepared by a charming native Californian."

Pleased that she could tell someone Derek would call, De-Ann turned sideways. Watching Julie spoon coffee into the percolator, she said, "By the way, if Derek should happen to phone this afternoon, I guess you better let me take it even if I'm busy." She had forced her speech to sound casual, though her stomach muscles were clenching with excitement just thinking about hearing his voice.

"He's going to phone here! Wow, he must really be zonkers about you. Isn't he a dream? I got goose bumps just seeing him walk in the door. He's so big and sexy-looking."

"Really? I never looked that closely but I guess he looks okay." She thought what a hypocrite she was to let Julie think she wasn't zonkers over him herself. De-Ann smiled impudently with smug satisfaction. Apparently she wasn't as old as she thought, remembering his sudden appearances had given her goose bumps too.

The morning passed swiftly. De-Ann completed the second page of the long menu. Merriment filled the room as her infectious laughter and exhilarated mood brightened Julie's placid disposition.

De-Ann sipped a cup of hot black coffee as she took a break just before lunchtime. Entering the front, she smiled softly. "Julie, when you finish that letter, why don't you go buy us a pizza? One with everything on it. Get a thick crust with lots of gooey cheese, pepperoni, mushrooms, sausage, and black olives."

Julie looked up in surprise. "That sounds delicious, De-Ann, but you rarely eat lunch. I didn't even know you liked pizza."

"I love it and today I'm starving." After taking her wallet from her purse, she handed Julie fifteen dollars. "Buy a large one, then you can take the leftovers home for a midnight snack."

Julie's eyes lit up at the thought of her and her husband sharing a snack after her babies were asleep. Thanking her boss profusely, she left, driving De-Ann's new car to purchase their lunch.

Seated in her comfortable office chair, De-Ann relaxed while the office was quiet. On a sheet of parchment she wrote Derek's name, idling her time, first printing in a flourish of Roman, followed by Italic script, Gothic–Old

English, Uncial, Eastern, and Oriental. Once in majuscules then again in minuscule letters. Admiring her work, she laughed, thinking she hadn't done that since having her first crush at thirteen.

When the phone rang, she deliberately counted four rings before picking up the receiver. "De-Ann's."

Without preamble Derek queried, "Secretary out?"

"Yes, why?" she answered indifferently, though her heart hammered uncontrollably at the first sound of his voice.

"Your office is so small that it shouldn't take over one ring to answer. Did I interrupt your work?"

"Actually yes. I was in the middle of printing a very important person's name."

"Mine?" he teased, unaware how disturbing his deep voice was.

"Certainly not!" she lied without a qualm.

"How does Chinese food sound?"

"Great. Why?" He would be surprised, she thought, to know that anything sounded fine if shared in his bracing company. "Are you taking me out to dinner again tonight?"

"Of course," he answered mischievously.

"Not 'of course' again. How do you know that I don't have other plans? You are assuming a lot, aren't you?" She chuckled, spoiling all attempts to sound haughty.

"I told you last night you were my property," Derek shot back, his voice suddenly serious. "I meant it, my De-Ann. I'm the only man in your life from now on."

Independent and uncowed, De-Ann flared back quickly. "Don't I have any say in the matter, Mr. Howell?"

"Of course not, Ms. Wagner."

"Darn, you're saying it again. I'll go to dinner with you but only because *I*—hear that?—*I* want to and I love Chinese food. But I warn you now, Mr. Derek Howell, that anytime I want to go out with someone else I will. I don't give a hoot what you think because I darn well won't ask your permission!" *Put that in your pipe and smoke it,* she thought with smug satisfaction.

"Don't try it, De-Ann. You will end up in my bed so fast, you'll think a hurricane hit town," he warned, his meaning emphatic.

Sensing the ruthlessness of his warning, she was astounded. His lighthearted bantering had changed the moment he thought she was serious about dating another man.

Inwardly she felt pleased by his possessiveness, and her lips raised in a wide smile before she chuckled out loud. "You sound like a great huge monster again, Mr. Howell. I guess I'd have some say about who I sleep with."

"Wouldn't like to wager on that, would you, minx?" he taunted.

"I don't bet," she sassed, picturing his deep frown and aggressive stance.

"Good, because you would lose. You're mine, and if you get too recalcitrant and quarrelsome, I'll damn well take you to my bed within the next hour."

"My, my, aren't you ill-tempered today? Guess I'd better soothe your weary brow and remain placid until you get in a better mood. Where do you want to pick me up? Here or my apartment?"

"Makes no difference. Did you take a taxi to work?"

"Yes."

"With my money?"

"No. I paid for the cab with my money but used yours to tip the driver. He was quite impressed with my generosity when I gave him a ten-dollar bill."

"*Your* generosity!" he snapped back, laughing loudly. "That was my money."

"I know. That's why I gave it to him. I told you I didn't want to feel like a kept woman."

"That does it! I have half a notion to leave my office, take you home, and give your ex-boyfriend Alan something to really be jealous of."

Giggling at Derek's sudden tirade, De-Ann hung up. She waited with hand poised to lift the receiver the moment he rang back. After the few seconds it took to redial, the phone rang.

"De-Ann's. Who's calling, please?" she taunted mischievously.

"Be in your office at six o'clock!" His adamant command was followed by a quick bang as he hung up on her.

De-Ann smiled, amused by his domineering ways, as she returned to work. Intent on finishing the menu before six, she looked up only briefly when Julie entered carrying a large flat carton. "Smells good but I'll pass. Derek's taking me to dinner again."

The secretary stood there, openmouthed but pleased by her boss's exuberant expression. She went to her desk, intent on skipping lunch too, but the spicy aroma of the rich pizza soon persuaded her. So, she thought, there would be two fewer slices for her and her husband's midnight feast.

Promptly at six Derek entered De-Ann's. His eyes narrowed as he saw her waiting for him in a lovely bright-colored dress. Her enticing face was exquisitely made up, her hair lustrous smooth around her shoulders.

Walking halfway to meet him, she held her wrist up to his nose. "Like it?" she asked impudently.

"What? Your wrist or that sexy perfume?"

"The perfume, of course. It cost a small fortune. My wrist is just a common body part," she added impertinently.

"Common? There's not a common body part on you."

Laughing at her flushed face, he bent forward to give her a brief kiss on her upraised mouth. Arm-in-arm they walked to his Ferrari.

De-Ann relaxed against the comfortable seat, smiling at Derek. "This is starting a bad habit. I'll get spoiled and won't ever want to cook at home."

"Surely you don't know how to cook too?"

"Of course. Darn, now you have me saying it."

"Just what can't you do?" he asked humorously.

"Lots of things. I can't fly a plane, scuba dive, build a house or . . . grow chin whiskers—"

"Enough! Enough!" Derek interrupted, his laughter filling the car. "I can do all those but I have to admit I'm particularly glad you can't do the last thing you mentioned. I wouldn't enjoy nuzzling my face against your smooth cheeks if I knew you had to shave twice a day too."

"You're a nut, Mr. Howell." A feeling of happiness surged through De-Ann as she watched him maneuver with calm expertise through the crowded streets of San Francisco's renowned Chinatown.

Hunger pangs gnawed at her empty stomach as he slid to a smooth stop. It had been hours since her light breakfast and she was starving. A possessive hand touched her waist as Derek guided her through the throngs of people into the colorful interior of his favorite Chinese restaurant. Shown to a choice table by the smiling hostess, they were seated and given a large ornate menu.

De-Ann observed the multitude of selections before looking at Derek. "Would you like to order? I'm not familiar with many of the dishes, other than chow mein and chop suey."

"Neither of which are from China, I'm sure you realize. They are supposed to have been invented right here in the nineteenth century."

"I knew that and I think they are both delicious."

"None of that tonight. I have plans to tutor you in a number of new delights throughout the next few weeks," he warned her, his darkened eyes making a quick survey of her voluptuous breasts. "Cuisine and—"

"Enough! Enough!" she scolded, this time interrupting his comments before he could voice his libidinous intentions.

Derek ordered with confidence, his ease in a variety of surroundings not surprising De-Ann in the least. He was casually dressed in white sport slacks and a deep blue body shirt that hugged his broad chest. He was devastatingly handsome, his presence dwarfing that of all the other men in the room.

"Happy?" he inquired after the waitress left. His hand slid forward to her fingers. Clasping them in his strong grip, he drew them to him. He turned her palm up and placed a searing kiss in the center.

De-Ann jerked away, his touch stirring her memories as it stirred her blood. A soft flush of color stained each cheek.

"Well?" he persisted, amused by her actions. "Are you?"

"Yes, Derek, I am. Extremely, but also old enough to be cautious. You come on pretty strong, and I'm determined not to be used like a cheap toy, then discarded without another thought. Let's keep our relationship cool . . . please!" she pleaded ineffectively.

"Cool! How in the hell could we keep what we feel for each other cool? Be honest with yourself, De-Ann. We strike sparks. Hot, searing sparks that ignite to a consuming flame the minute we touch. Cool!" He laughed in exasperation, his throaty voice lowered to a deep intimate sound. "I think not, my love, as you shall see. Now drink your tea," he commanded, filling the tiny cup.

De-Ann lowered her head, watching the swirling tea leaves settle in the amber liquid as she pondered his earnest declaration. Adding a small amount of sugar, she stirred it thoughtfully.

"I won't be coerced into anything I don't want, Derek —including your much-used bed," she blurted out candidly.

"By 'much used,' you mean a variety of women, I presume?"

"Yes. Your reputation is not that of a saint."

"I realize that, and it's founded on fact. I see no reason to deny my interest in women. I have strong needs and manage to assuage them easily. You have strong needs too, De-Ann," he told her bluntly. "Yours are just surfacing later in life than mine. Believe me, when you are fully awakened, you won't be satisfied living a barren life as you do now either."

"My Lord, you don't pull any punches, do you?" she retorted, upset that he might be correct. Already she was anticipating the moment when they were alone and she was clasped firmly in his arms, her mouth crushed beneath his firm, sensuous lips.

"Not with you I don't. We have been honest about our feelings from the first and I want it to continue that way. There will be no deceit between us."

He took a sip of tea before setting the cup on the table, his eyes narrowing as he held her glance. "Understand one thing, De-Ann. You are the first woman who lay in my bed. I never make love in my home. A first-class hotel is much more preferable. I have never wanted friendship or permanent ties with my companions. Only release from my physical needs and satisfaction of theirs."

De-Ann shook her head, a feeling of hot jealousy running through her for the first time in her life. "I don't want to hear about it!" she blurted out angrily. "You sound so casual, as if it was no different from eating or sleeping to restore your energy."

"It was casual. No emotion on either side, I assure you."

Interrupted by their waitress, they watched as an endless assortment of stainless steel bowls was placed before them. De-Ann, pleased by her intrusion, watched as she lifted the lids, explaining what each dish was. The tension of their disturbing conversation ended as De-Ann and Derek heaped their plates with a portion of each dish.

"I hope you don't expect me to eat with chopsticks?" she asked anxiously.

"Not if you don't want to. It's really quite simple once you learn the proper technique of holding them and moving your fingers. Here, let me show you." Laughing at her first awkward attempts, he told her, "You better practice at home. Your dinner will get cold if you don't use a fork tonight."

De-Ann agreed, laying her chopsticks on the cloth. Undecided which to taste first, she admired the excellently prepared meal.

Ch'ao Lung Hsia, luscious lobster Cantonese; *T'an Ts'u Chu Jo,* batter fried sweet and sour pork in a tantalizing sauce; *Ssu Chi Tou Niu Ju,* beef with crisp green beans in tangy marinade; *Hsing Jen Chi Ting,* diced chicken with almonds; *Ca'ao Fan,* fried rice; *Wu Dep Har,* butterfly shrimp in a featherlight batter; *Wu Hsiang Ya,* spiced duck cooked with sherry and soy sauce.

De-Ann's stomach ached from the amount of delicious food she had consumed. She sat back in her chair, hands holding her middle as she laughed. "I'm absolutely stuffed. You'll have me fat in a month."

"You could use a few more pounds, De-Ann," he remarked honestly. She was slender, her slim limbs emphasizing her full breasts and rounded hips. "In an hour you'll beg me for a hamburger."

"Oh, don't mention food now," she groaned, smiling as he pushed his plate aside also. "We've been eating and talking for hours."

Derek motioned for their waitress and asked her to place the vast amount of leftovers in cartons for them to take home.

"You surprise me, Derek. I never expected you to be thrifty."

"In many ways I am, but this is not for me. It's for you. I'm flying to Florida tomorrow and I want to assure myself that you'll eat a proper dinner. We had enough left to feed you for a week. There was no need to waste it."

Dejected by his news, she remained silent, fingers nervously clasping her empty teacup.

"I'm looking at property. I'll be back a week from Saturday. If the weather's nice, we'll go to Fisherman's Wharf for the day."

Derek was handed their bill along with a plate holding two fortune cookies. "Open it and read it to me," he asked, handing her the crisp cookie.

De-Ann cracked it open. Reading her fortune, she chuckled, eyes sparkling like precious jewels as they met Derek's. "It says I will meet a tall, dark stranger."

"That's me. Since we have already met, the prophecy is four days late. Let's see what mine says." He broke his cookie, read his fortune, and started to laugh as he handed her the tiny white paper to read.

She scanned it quickly, giggling happily. "This could never happen again. But what will you do with a tall, dark stranger too?"

"Well, since I wouldn't be interested in a woman my height, I'd send her on her way. As for a man, that isn't worth mentioning."

Derek grabbed her hand and held it gently. "I have no use for any woman now other than the one with jade-colored eyes with mysterious depths and rich auburn hair that glimmers in all light."

"A very poetic statement, Mr. Howell," she said, savoring his flattering attention.

He paid their bill, gathered the sack of leftovers in one arm, and escorted her to his car. De-Ann started to get in as he opened the passenger door, only to be stopped by his hand.

"Not yet. We, my young woman, are going to take a walking tour of Chinatown. I just wanted to put your dinner in the backseat."

"Wonderful. After that meal I need the exercise."

Derek took her hand, dwarfing it in his palm. They started walking up the crowded sidewalks. Content, she listened attentively as he explained its picturesque history.

"With the exception of Singapore, more Chinese live in our Chinatown than in any other place in the world outside of China. It covers approximately sixteen square blocks and is known as a city within a city. A colorful addition to San Francisco."

Hand-in-hand they strolled the well-lighted streets. They took their time, looking at interesting temples, shops packed from floor to ceiling with goods for sale, tearooms with inviting decor, Christian missions, schools, theaters, and grocery stores filled with unique condiments, and opened cartons of fruits and vegetables haphazardly stacked out front on the crowded sidewalks.

After returning to the car, De-Ann leaned against the soft leather upholstery with a weary sigh. "That was a wonderful walk. I fell in love with the tiny little Bank of Canton. It was dwarfed by its neighbors, but they didn't get a second glance. Not with its fascinating curled eaves,

71

and shiny brass ornamentation. But, gosh, don't the streets seem steep and narrow here?"

"Yes, they do, but it was fun, wasn't it?" he agreed, pulling from the curb. "You know something? You're the first girl I have ever held hands with. Surprised?"

"Hmm . . . yes. You led an unusual childhood. I remember the first boy to hold my hand was five years old. Little Bernard Derryberry. He was an intense young man with horn-rimmed glasses and kinky blond hair, and stood half a foot shorter than me. We declared our love for each other continually."

"Well, I'll be damned," he growled in a pretense at jealousy, his eyes alight with good humor. "What happened to him?"

"We broke up," she said matter-of-factly. "I hit him in the nose when he wouldn't loan me his shoelace to lead a stray dog home with. His mother was so incensed by her son's bloody nose, she forbid me to play with him for a month. By then I had other interests."

"You were a minx even then, I gather."

"Definitely. My hair was a bright carrot-red, my temper quick, and disposition fearless. My poor parents were to be pitied."

Derek glanced at her profile as he pulled to a stop in front of her apartment.

"I find it hard to imagine your glorious mane of hair anything other than dark auburn."

As they walked to her apartment he took her key, then opened the door as he had the previous night. De-Ann set her purse down, kicking off her high-heeled sandals first thing. She took the cartons of Chinese food to her kitchen and transferred them to plastic containers for the freezer before turning to Derek, who had followed her.

"Coffee, tea, or—"

"You!" he broke into her conversation, his broad frame dwarfing the small room.

"I was not the third choice! I was going to ask if you would like a drink, though. I have a well-stocked cupboard and you're welcome to help yourself."

Derek opened the appropriate cupboard door to see four bottles of liquor. He smiled, thinking of his home's wine cellar with its cases of aged bourbon, vodka, gin, and vintage champagne that he kept to entertain frequent guests. His wine list was one of the most extensive private collections in the city. He took a bottle of whiskey from her cupboard, looking around for glasses. After pouring the first drink, he added ice and handed it to De-Ann.

"No, thanks, Derek. I rarely drink." At his puzzled expression she explained, "That night Alan was celebrating passing his bar exam and I'm afraid I got carried away helping him." She plugged in the percolator, looking forward to a long evening in his company while she sipped her favorite brew.

"That was my lucky night," he told her gently. After drinking his whiskey in one long gulp, he set the glass on the counter and led her back into the living room. He sat down on the velour sofa, drawing her close, his arm around her shoulder, hips touching.

"Snuggle close, sweetheart. I want you to be sweet and loving for the next hour, then I have to leave. I won't see you for eleven days and I don't want you to provoke me by starting an argument or asserting your womanly views on equality between the sexes."

"But I haven't!" she retorted, leaning her head against the comfort of his wide shoulder.

"I know," he murmured, content to enfold her in his arm and fondle the slender smoothness of her shoulder.

"Why, darn you, Derek. That's unfair," she fumed.

"There you go." Checking his watch, he laughed.

"Fifty-eight seconds and you're already asserting your emancipation."

De-Ann clenched her lips together, deciding to sit for one full hour without saying a single word. *See how you like that,* she scolded him silently. Not one word would she utter until he left.

Derek laughed inwardly at her mutinous expression. Ignoring her, he talked about his youth, college days, and the complexities of his northern California land development.

His fingers stroked the heavy strands of silky hair, stopping intermittently to caress her shoulders while he talked. He felt smug, satisfied with her reaction, as she cuddled closer and listened intently. When he purposely quizzed her about her childhood, she forgot her intentions of teaching him a lesson and within minutes was relating many amusing incidents of her youth.

It was apparent with each word that De-Ann had come from a totally different environment with loving parents who guided her with a gentle hand. Her deep moral values and sense of independence were instilled in her as a young child. Entranced, Derek felt a strange peace settle over him, conscious that he ached to know each detail that made up her total personality.

Unthinkingly De-Ann reached her hand to his thigh. She felt the muscles tighten beneath her touch. Feeling embarrassed, she pulled her trailing fingers away and glanced through her dark lashes at his face. Mesmerized by his intense expression, she leaned across his chest, lips parted, waiting for his kiss.

"Are you a tease?"

"Of course not," she declared, her voice muffled as she lay her head on his chest. Her heart beat rapidly at the feel of his body's warmth and the clean smell that invaded her nostrils.

"Running your finger up my leg then removing it was teasing."

"I'm sorry. I wasn't even aware what I was doing. To be truthful, most of the things I do with you I'm not conscious of until after I've done them," she apologized, her arms clinging to his lean waist as she continued to rest on his chest.

"Don't be sorry for whatever you do to me," he said, his voice thickened with desire. "But be prepared to take the consequences."

"Such as?" she taunted, squirming to get closer.

"This!" Derek pushed her back so she lay full length along the couch, his eyes dark and serious with warning.

She raised her arms to his nape, gentle hands clasping his strong neck. "Derek . . . kiss me," she whispered, ready to seek the touch of his lips even if she had to beseech him.

"One good-bye kiss only," he murmured, his voice soft as velvet as he lowered his body over hers. His hips pressed her unresisting form deep into the soft cushions.

The weight of his taut body brought an aching need deep within her. She could feel the contrast of his hard arms and legs as they entwined with her own softer feminine limbs. Her breasts were briefly crushed beneath the strength of his powerful chest, but she made no protest. He rose to prop himself up on his elbows and cupped her face, his expression tender.

"One will do," she whispered breathlessly, entranced by his touch.

His eyes devoured her face as his lips ached to do to her generous mouth. Prolonging the emotion-charged moment before first contact, he told her, "You are beautiful, De-Ann. Beautiful to look at and beautiful to touch."

Derek's body trembled against hers—the actions of a sensual man holding himself too long from his deepest desires. His head lowered, his mouth caressing hers lightly, his firm lips exploring hers. He tasted her as a gourmet would his finest meal, knowing his hunger was fast becoming insatiable.

His kiss deepened, parting her mouth to savor its entirety with his questing tongue. His hands slid from her side to the buttons of her dress. Deft fingers opened the bodice, exposing the velvety skin of one full breast to his palm.

Derek raised up, enabling his mouth to follow the path of his hands. He trailed his lips along her neck to the pulsating hollow of her throat. He kissed the sensitive skin with slow expertise, aroused by the sound of excited throaty murmurs beneath his lips.

De-Ann's attempts to ward off his seeking mouth were futile. She knew to fight him would be to fight herself. Without protest she let her body's needs guide her. She pressed his head to her breasts, her slender, capable fingers threaded in the raven-black waves of hair. She arched upward to meet the initial touch of his lips on her curves.

Gasping as the volatile pleasure of his mouth moving over her sensitive skin intensified, she squirmed to get closer. His tongue stimulated her rose-pink nipple until it was a hard, throbbing bud. Moist and warm, his mouth continued its erotic teasing, covering all the ivory perfection of her full breast.

Soft whimpers escaped her throat at the evocative exploration. She pushed helplessly against his wide shoulders. The surging motion of his mouth was devastating, stirring her to unbearable ecstasy.

"No! No . . . please, I can't stand any more." Teardrops slid down her cheeks unchecked. Tears of embarrassment that she had let him touch her intimately. Tears of rapture from the pleasure she felt.

Derek raised his hardened body from her instantly. He drew her into his arms, cradling her against his chest, voice low and hypnotic as he crooned soothingly, "Hush, my darling. Don't cry. This is how you should always be with me, how I fantasized you would respond. Never be ashamed of your feelings when I arouse you."

De-Ann bit back tears, looking at his intelligent face with eyes that shimmered in the dim lamplight. "It's not your fault, Derek. I don't blame you for anything. I asked to be kissed and waited all night to feel your impersonal touches turn to caresses."

She lay quiescent, letting the enchantment of his hands pacify her banked desires. His fingers glided through her tousled hair and over her back, bringing her bliss wherever he lingered.

"I wasn't prepared for so much emotional havoc, Derek. It's inconceivable that I could become so carried away by my own passions that I would let you—a man I have only known four days—fondle me without protest."

"Fondle you?" he questioned raggedly, his eyes loving as he bent to kiss the lustrous hair in disarray across her forehead.

"For lack of a more suitable word," she explained, her cheeks flushing.

"I was making love to you. Passionate love, sweetheart, that has just started. You have much to experience, De-Ann, and for the first time in my life I am willing to wait. Each new sensual happening for you will be a delight for me."

As she started to raise herself from the intimacy of his touch, he stopped her. "Let me." His hands gently buttoned the front of her dress after pulling the lace-edged cup of her bra over the enticing sight of her naked breast.

His hard knuckles against her skin started the familiar churning in her stomach. She resisted the impulse to hold his hand to her body. When he had finished, she stood up on unsteady legs. Fighting for composure, she suddenly

77

recalled making coffee earlier. A short moment by her watch but a long time in maturity.

"Would you like some coffee before you go?"

"Please. I take it black. I have had enough sweet-tasting things tantalize my palate during the last several minutes."

"I'm no honey pot," she shot back quickly. Slow to regain her composure, she was swift to regain her impetuous tongue.

"Not much you aren't. You are an entire beehive," he told her in a voice tinged with amusement. With his hand on her waist he led her to the kitchen. Derek took down two cups and poured their coffee. They stood, deep in thought, drinking the hot brew. Both needed the diversion from their real desires.

Taking a long drink, they looked up at the same time. Their laughter joined in the small kitchen as they saw the humor in the situation.

De-Ann's eyes glimmered with mirth as she teased Derek. "We are both doing things we have never done before. I am fast losing my morals and you are beginning to get some."

"You little devil. That was uncalled for. Just because I leave your chastity belt intact you think I am improving?"

"You bet! According to my secretary you usually don't leave a path of virgins as you travel down the highway of life."

"Now who's being poetic . . . and corny, I might add. Tell your secretary not to believe everything she reads. Most, but not all!" His voice sobered, telling her, "I've yet to take a virgin."

Derek set his empty coffee cup on the counter before cupping her slender shoulders. His head bent to place a brief kiss on De-Ann's temple. A fleeting kiss implying great reverence.

"I'll be back Friday night late. Be waiting at ten o'clock Saturday morning and we will continue this interesting discussion."

Leaving the kitchen, he paused to look over his shoulder. "Don't get too smug about thinking you are teaching me moral values, De-Ann. It's easier to slip than it is to climb, so beware."

De-Ann laughed, knowing that again Derek had had the final word. After washing the cups, she walked into the living room and heard the sound of his Ferrari pulling from the curb. The noise was followed by total silence. The sudden loss of noise that an empty room had when the person who had filled it with happiness had left.

Without surprise she noticed a ten-dollar bill laying on her table. Her taxi fare to work the next day.

She prepared for bed in a glow of contentment, yet she was aware that she would have to take the consequences if their relationship went beyond her strict principles of right and wrong. Derek had shown her that he was willing to let her set the limits.

She climbed into her single bed and stretched out indolently. Her wary mind in a quandary, she closed her eyes and thought out loud, "Mother dear, you didn't warn me about men whose one touch sets your blood on fire."

CHAPTER FIVE

"Gee, De-Ann, can you believe it's already Friday?" Julie asked as she gathered her purse from her desk drawer prior to going home.

"Can I ever!" De-Ann replied instantly. "The last ten long days have dragged." She handed Julie her paycheck, watching as she read the amount.

"Wow! Why so much?"

"I just thought you might enjoy a twenty-five-dollar-a-week raise. The cost of everything is increasing so rapidly and two young babies have to be expensive." She smiled, pleased by her young secretary's excited face.

"Thanks, De-Ann," Julie said sincerely. "You gave me a raise only three months ago, and I really don't do all that much. You were terrific to hire me in the first place, since I didn't have any experience."

"You've managed fine, Julie. You're honest, reliable, and your typing has improved tremendously. What more could I want?" De-Ann complimented her, amused as her young face flushed with pride.

"I better rush or I'll miss my bus. Jimmie expects his

dinner on the dot of seven. Maybe he'll take me and the kids to the park tomorrow to celebrate my raise."

"Sounds like fun. I hope the weather is bright and sunny."

"Are you—er, is Mr. Howell, going to take you somewhere?" Julie asked curiously, wondering why her boss hadn't mentioned his name for several days.

De-Ann's eyes darkened to jade as she whispered dreamily. "Yes, we're going to spend the day exploring Fisherman's Wharf. Derek has been to Florida on business and returns late tonight."

"That's why your days have passed so slow then," she spoke without thinking. "Sorry, I didn't mean to be impertinent."

"That's okay, and I do believe you are right." De-Ann laughed at Julie's remark, telling her to have a nice weekend as she left for the corner bus stop. As was her normal routine on Friday, De-Ann straightened her office, checked that the plants were watered, put her work supplies in their proper place, and cleared her desktop.

Purse in hand, she secured the door, unlocked her Mazda, and drove to her residence, all accomplished with thoughts of Derek's returning foremost in her mind. She kicked off her shoes the minute she entered her cool apartment, setting her purse down with a sigh of relief, glad to be home.

She walked to the kitchen, took down the coffee, prepared the percolator, and plugged it in automatically. The soft *plop, plop* sound as the water started bubbling was drowned out by her joyful voice humming as she anticipated the following day.

She took the last plastic container of frozen Chinese food from the freezer. She emptied it into a small pan and placed it on the stove to simmer before walking to her bedroom.

Half an hour later, freshly bathed, shampooed hair wrapped in a soft towel to dry, and wearing her favorite silk robe, she sat on the couch. Feet tucked comfortably under her, she watched the evening news, enjoying her dinner as she relaxed. The smell of fresh-perked coffee overpowered the steaming sweet and sour pork on her plate.

She went to bed at midnight, excitement welling in her breast that in ten hours she would see Derek. Derek Howell, who had tormented her thoughts each day that he had been away.

She was awakened from a sound sleep by a heavy knocking on the front door. She turned on her bedside lamp to check the clock, alarmed when she saw it was only three in the morning. Her heart pounded with fear as the loud noise continued. Fumbling with clumsy fingers, she slipped into her robe, fearing something must have happened to her mother. Her face was pale as she rushed to the door.

Without caution De-Ann opened it the width the chain lock would allow, then, tears coming to her eyes, slipped the safety catch.

Letting out a happy cry at the sight of him, she threw her arms around Derek's slim waist as he entered her apartment, kicking the door shut behind him. Her freshly washed hair tumbled about her shoulders in disarray. Her face was free of makeup, she wore only nightwear, but she held him as if they were longtime lovers who had been parted for months.

"Why are you here at this hour?" she questioned, her voice a throaty sound muffled against his broad chest.

"Kiss me, De-Ann," he moaned raggedly, his arms crushing her supple body ardently. Aroused by the feel of her naked curves clad in a thin silk nightgown and robe, he raised her chin with eagerness. His eyes lingered on each detail of her exquisite sleep-softened face before his mouth slowly lowered to hers.

"One good-morning kiss only," she murmured affectionately, her body arching upward so she could reach his lips.

"One will do, my darling, one will do." Her toes barely touched the carpeting as he pulled her into his arms to claim her lips.

His mouth molded to hers in a demanding, possessive kiss, fiercer than his previous kisses. The hunger in his body ran through hers like wildfire, consuming her with its barely controlled passion.

She gloried in his hands that moved over her back in slow, even strokes before stopping, fingers spread possessively across the base of her spine. Pressed against the length of his body, she felt him harden with desire, and knew he was as aroused by her touch as she was by his. As he reluctantly released her mouth, his face buried in her tousled hair, she whispered softly, "Has it been only ten days?"

Pleased that De-Ann was so sensitive to the emptiness of their time apart, Derek murmured into her ear, his tongue probing the tantalizing cavity, "Eleven days, sweetheart. It is Saturday now and I left Wednesday. Eleven long days of abstinence."

De-Ann wrapped her arms around his neck. Threading her fingers through the crisp dark hair, she gave a sharp tug.

"Abstinence makes the heart grow fonder," she told him smugly, chuckling at his look of consternation as he pulled back.

"Good Lord, I'm crazy about an early morning comedienne!" He gave her a sharp pat on the firm contours of her buttocks, amused as she broke into a loud giggle.

She withdrew from his hold to stand before him. Her

eyes were bright with happiness as she scanned his face, one hand holding the tousled waves of hair from her face, the other on the lapels of her robe. "How was your trip?"

"Fine. I'll tell you about it later."

"Why did you come by here, then?"

Derek placed his hands on her shoulders and took her parted lips in a brief hard kiss. "That's why. I couldn't wait until ten o'clock to do that."

"You're crazy!" she retorted impudently. But her lips betrayed her as they raised in a smile.

"About you," he growled deep in his throat, eyes leering as they mischievously lingered on her soft curves visible beneath the clinging silk.

"I have something for you," he told her, suddenly solemn.

"What?"

"This." Derek went out the front door, then returned carrying a gigantic spray of red roses. Dozens of dark flowers were arranged in a white wicker basket with REST IN PEACE written in gold letters on the wide ribbon stretched across the curved handle.

De-Ann's mouth opened as she stared at the funeral spray. "Oh, no! You didn't take it off someone's burial plot, did you?" she asked, appalled at the thought.

"Of course not," Derek scolded. "How dare you even think I would do such a thing." He placed the basket against the bay window in the front of her living room before turning around. "This, my suspicious beauty, came from the only florist I could find open in San Francisco at this hour. Quite a good buy too, considering the number of red roses it contains. Seems that the person it was ordered for didn't die after all, thus your fortune and my bargain price."

"Go home, Derek. You're insane, and I need my sleep

84

if I'm going to put up with a day of your exclusive company."

His broad palms held her motionless as his head lowered. Inhaling the heady scent of her skin, he rained gentle kisses along her smooth neck, his heart beating erratically.

"Can I stay?" he moaned, his voice deep and sensuous.

"No!" She could feel the hunger in his body and hear it in his voice. It took all her willpower to resist, but she felt relieved by his quick admission.

"I thought not. That's the curse of falling for a virgin. Enjoy it, honey. I'm not a patient man and you won't be one much longer."

"I don't know. I think I'll have the final say about that!"

"I agree," he whispered in her ear, his lips continuing to nibble a fiery path along her neck, his hands holding her still in their firm grip.

"Y-you do?" she questioned breathlessly, his mouth working magic wherever it touched.

"Of course." Derek's face raised, his glance serious as he held her eyes. "But then I would be a poor lover if I couldn't seduce you into begging me to take you anytime I set my hands and mouth—er—mind to it."

"That does it," she retorted, scolding him firmly. Her breasts rose and fell rapidly; her stormy expression showed disapproval over his blatant remarks.

Derek watched her, his blue eyes darkening with fascination. She stood before him proudly, eyes flashing, chin raised defiantly, both hands on her hips. "You're beautiful when you're mad. Your fiery little face, that tousled red hair, and heaving bosom are enough to make me lose sleep the rest of the morning," he exclaimed fervently.

"Out! Out of this apartment right now, Derek Howell."

Laughing at her rebellion, he gave her pouting lips one last kiss. Then he left, shutting the door with deliberate

85

indolence, his head held arrogantly as he leaped down the stairs to his waiting car.

"Fool," she scolded herself aloud. "But I love you, Mr. Howell." Shocked by her sudden declaration, De-Ann knew it was true. She had fallen in love, heedless of his deep cynicism. At that moment she was uncaring of anything but that he returned her feelings with equal concern.

Removing her robe, De-Ann climbed into bed. She was soon asleep for the second time, a single red rosebud clutched in one hand. At peace knowing Derek was safe, she slept soundly until daylight.

Dressed, makeup applied, hair brushed to a lustrous sheen, she waited. She was adding another subtle spray of her favorite perfume to her throat and wrist when she heard Derek's rapid knocking. Smiling at his boyish impatience, she walked to her living room.

"You're an hour early." She smiled, stepping aside to let him in.

"I know. I was hoping to catch you lying in bed. Spending the day there sounded better to me than tromping all around the wharf." His eyes lingered on her outfit. "You look gorgeous."

"Thank you for the compliment. This is the first time you've seen me in slacks."

"I've seen you without them," he reminded her, laughing as she flushed. "You have a perfect figure, sweetheart. Slim shapely legs outlined in green slacks." His hands clasped her narrow waist, his long fingers touching. "Handspan waist." He let them slide up her rib cage to cup the swell of her breasts.

She jerked from his teasing touch, rebuking him firmly, "My blouse is a green and rust paisley silk, and you don't have to touch me to describe the rest of my figure."

"Darn. I was just getting to where I wanted to linger," he teased. He took her hand, his mood turning serious as

86

he pulled her to his side. Inhaling the heady fragrance of her perfume, he told her, "You smell sweet and clean. Like a bouquet."

"That's the funeral spray you smell."

"The hell you say. That's your skin. Your delicious, delectable, silky skin."

Reaching for a large brown shoulder bag that matched her comfortable low-heeled leather sandals, she scolded, "Hush, Derek, you're beginning to sound like a pervert. I decided after you left this morning that today would be spent in totally platonic behavior." She waited for his fierce denial. He surprised her again by shrugging his broad shoulders agreeably.

"Whatever you want, honey." Placing her sweater over one arm, he escorted her down the stairs to his gleaming Ferrari.

The morning air was brisk, typical of San Francisco, but the sky was clear with the promise of a beautiful afternoon ahead. Derek drove to the wharf, parking in an all-day parking lot. He guided her across the pavement to the loading area for the red-and-white-fleet bay cruise, his hand resting with proprietorship on her waist.

De-Ann stopped, shaking her head as she looked up. "I've already been on this, Derek, so save your money."

"You haven't been on it with me. Anything you experienced with anyone else doesn't count. From now on only what we do together will be important." He purchased the tickets, grabbed her hand, and led her aboard among the waiting multitude of sightseers.

"Egotist!" she chided beneath her breath, hoping no one else could hear. "Stubborn, arrogant, chauvinistic egotist!"

Derek guided her to the bow of the large boat. Then, pinching her waist with a sharp nip, he whispered in her ear, "I heard that, minx, and you'll pay for each word later today."

Hidden by the large group of people wandering around deciding where to sit, she kicked his shin. Defiantly she turned her back on him and walked to the stairway that led to the top deck. The boat moved sluggishly as it pulled with care from the dock. She shivered as the damp air hit her arms. The breeze whipped her hair around her face.

"Put this on or you'll catch cold," Derek spoke behind her.

De-Ann's eyes fell on the sweater he held out to her, then met his. "It took you long enough to follow me. I thought I would freeze to death," she said impudently.

"You little devil. You damn near broke my other leg today." He turned her around to help her on with the sweater, then gathered her into his arms from behind. She felt the warmth of his huge body seep into her chilled limbs with delicious pleasure. Feeling small and protected, she leaned back, her hands clasping his as they crossed over her waist.

De-Ann cocked her head sideways, looking at Derek out of the corner of her eye. "You make a good substitute for a jacket, although I think a full-length mink coat would be preferable."

"Why?" he murmured against her windblown hair, the sound of his voice nearly drowned out by the boat's motors and the deep water of the bay breaking across the bow.

"Because I could keep a coat in my bedroom and it wouldn't bother me!"

"You're really asking for it today, De-Ann. I should let you stand here and freeze to death in this cold morning breeze but you're too good a windbreak and I like to stand outside rather than sit behind the windows."

"Windbreak! That's not very flattering. I thought you

were holding me to keep me warm, and it's only to keep your own big burly body from freezing."

"Hush."

"Why?"

"Because I am going to tell you a little of the city's history, whether you've heard it or not."

De-Ann turned around within his hold, hugging his waist. She burrowed her small face into his chest, watching sideways across the bay. The brisk wind tousled her hair, blowing silky strands across Derek's face as they stood on the heaving deck of the boat.

With both hands crossed behind her slender back, Derek lowered his head so she could easily hear. "To my right is Alcatraz Island. Have you taken the guided tour? The National Park Service gives a remarkably informative talk."

De-Ann shook her head no, keeping her face snuggled against his hard chest, aware that she was enjoying the closeness of their bodies more than the exhilarating cruise circling the bay.

"Pay attention and quit rubbing my waist or I'll be a physical wreck before we dock."

Looking at the bleak twelve-acre rock with its crumbling prison, De-Ann shuddered, thinking of the violent men it had housed. Notorious, hardened criminals were sent there, normally for life, as the isolation and strong currents of the bay made it virtually escape-proof. A brief twenty-nine-year period ended when it was closed in 1963.

The noise of the churning propellers was muffled when the swell of the incoming tide surged across the bow head on. Braced against Derek's broad strength, De-Ann clung to keep her balance when the boat lurched upward before coming down with a sharp bump.

Derek laughed out loud, his face expressing enjoyment

over the rough ride. Hugging De-Ann tightly, he teased, "Haven't got your sea legs yet, have you?"

Looking upward to his great height, the brisk wind blowing strands of her hair across his chest, she admitted the last tour had not been so rough. "I love it, though," she told him, thinking it made a fine excuse to stay in his arms.

"Good, but turn around now and grip the edge of the railing. I want you to see the Golden Gate Bridge as we approach it from this angle. It's entirely different from driving across the top."

De-Ann turned. The security of Derek's palms never left her waist until she was clinging to the smooth protective barrier. He stood behind her, encircling her body with strong sinewy arms.

A group of young students crowded and jostled each other coming to the bow, their happy cries and loud talk making De-Ann and Derek's attempt at conversation impossible.

Words weren't necessary as they stared at the grandeur of the fast-approaching span of the rust-colored bridge that connected San Francisco with Marin County and the Redwood Highway.

Derek lowered his head, nuzzling wind-whipped strands of silky hair from De-Ann's ear. He spoke huskily, tasting the salty spray that clung to her flushed cheeks. "You are a delight to me, darling. I've never met a woman who would stand on the bow of a boat and let the damp ocean breeze muss her hair."

Turning her face to look at him over her shoulder, she retorted quickly, "You've met all the wrong kind, then, Derek. I adore it and can't remember when I've felt better."

"I can," he teased, nipping the lobe of her ear sharply. "You felt better when you were naked on my bed, kissed me in your office, hugged me wearing only your silk night-gown and thin robe—"

De-Ann interrupted him with a sharp slap on his hand. "Hush, Derek, those kids might hear you," she warned, chuckling.

"Those kids, my sweet innocent, have probably done things that you don't even know about yet. They look like a pretty precocious group to me," he taunted, watching their rambunctious antics out of the corner of his eye.

"Takes one to know one, Mr. Howell."

Derek removed one hand from the railing to put around her waist. He squeezed sharply until she squirmed away to stand beside him.

The loud giggling subsided as the group went to the port side of the ship to look at the beauty of the shoreline and the towering buildings of the downtown area.

Derek commanded her attention as he started to speak. "Listen to me, De-Ann. I want you to be able to converse intelligently about our beautiful city."

"Why, you egotistical—"

"Hush, minx," he commanded, his voice a husky baritone as he looked at her with a serious expression.

Noticing the admiration in his eyes as they surged beneath the bridge, she stopped teasing and waited for him to continue.

"That's better. I like quiet women . . . sometimes! Did you know that the Golden Gate Bridge has an overall length of 8,981 feet and a main span length of 4,200 feet, making it one of the longest single-span suspension bridges ever built?"

"No."

"Did you know that its two massive towers are the world's highest bridge towers and are 746 feet above the water? That the largest oceangoing ships can pass beneath its clearance of 220 feet?"

"No." Proud of his knowledge, she asked, "Why do you remember these statistics?"

"Being a contractor and land developer, I'm interested in all things having to do with construction. I'm also keen with mathematics and seem to remember anything with figures in it." Eyeing her pert curves as he leaned back, he held his chin with one hand, dark blue eyes narrowing.

"I'd say you measure about—"

"Fool! You don't have to get personal," she interrupted. "My measurements have nothing to do with construction."

"You think not! My God, you've the most beautifully constructed lines I've ever seen. The symmetry of your figure defies the finest architect's ability to reproduce. An artist or sculpture would remain entranced for days attempting to depict so perfect a model."

"Flattery will get you everywhere, Mr. Howell," she mocked.

"Good. We'll go straight to my home when we dock."

"You didn't let me finish. I was going to say but not with me." Shivering as the chill finally penetrated despite her sweater and his broad body, she unconsciously pushed closer to him, seeking his warmth.

"Come on." Hand in hand they walked toward the stairs to the lower, enclosed deck. After making certain she was seated comfortably with a view of the shoreline, he left. She watched as they passed the U.S. Presidio and Fort Point National Historic site.

A smile of appreciation lit her face when Derek reappeared, deftly balancing two steaming cups of black coffee.

She sipped the hot liquid, sighing with pleasure as it warmed her chilled body. He sat beside her on the wooden seat, his hip touching hers, his arm casually draped around her shoulder. The nearness of Derek filled her with a different kind of warmth.

"We've got another half hour of the cruise left. Let's stay right here, okay?"

"Wonderful. As soon as I finish this delicious coffee, I'll brush my hair. I bet I look like a wild woman, don't I?"

Leaning back, he scanned the healthy color in her cheeks, the dark jade eyes that shimmered with excitement, and the auburn hair, vibrant and tousled sensuously. He refused to say a word, just sat there, grinning.

"Well?"

"Well, what?"

"Do I look okay?"

"Kind of like a scarecrow after a hard winter in the field." At De-Ann's sudden look of dismay he added casually, "Some men kind of like your type of look."

"Do you?"

"Hmmm . . . you're beginning to grow on me."

"Why, you monster, your hair is pretty messed up too!"

"Do I look okay?" He laughed mischievously.

Getting back at him, she shrugged one shoulder before glancing at him in a disinterested manner. "Some women kind of like your type of look."

"Do you?"

"Hmmm . . . you could begin to grow on me if I were susceptible."

His head lowered, his lips brushed her silky hair. "You little devil. You never need to ask if you look okay to me. I'm wild about you and you know it."

"Good. Tell me more about our city, then I'll tell you some things even you might not know."

"Okay, here's for starters. San Francisco is the nation's third largest port. The West Coast's largest saltwater marsh. The Bay is four hundred square miles and has two hundred seventy-six miles of shoreline."

"That's more statistics. Did you know it was the city's bayside location that lured its early colonizers? That in the late seventeen hundreds a European settlement was established at the Presidio at the end of the peninsula? During that same year the Franciscan Fathers founded a mission, and halfway between the Presidio and the mission a halting place named El Paraje de Yerba Buena sprang up. The 'Place of the Good Herb' is now near what's Portsmouth Square. The tiny town was later to be called San Francisco."

They stared at the beauty of the cosmopolitan city with its massive skyscrapers and the pyramid shape of the Transamerica Tower topping the skyline. It was hard to believe that in such a short time the early settlement of one hundred inhabitants had grown to a city of over seven hundred thousand people.

"Yes, but it wasn't until the discovery of gold in the American River that the city was inundated with thousands of hopefuls from all over the world who came seeking their fortune through its 'golden gates.' When the gold rush was over, most of them returned to the city, many more disappointed than successful."

Watching as a gull swooped by their window to land near a feeding white pelican, De-Ann thought of all the sea birds, the colorful beauty of each species, separate and distinct. Her eyes raised to Derek as she offered a sudden insight.

"It's the ethnic diversity that contributes to San Francisco's character and cultural sophistication, isn't it, Derek?"

He nodded in agreement, his lips raised in a smile. "Yes, we have large settlements of all races." Then as he stroked her hair, helping her smooth it as she combed the tumbled waves, he inserted, "Have you heard about the reign of Emperor Norton?"

"No. I've only lived here three years and I've been busy since I first opened my shop." Putting her comb back in her purse and applying a fresh application of glossy lipstick, she listened attentively.

"In 1859 he declared himself Emperor of the United States and Protector of Mexico. For twenty or so years he ruled this city, which tolerantly indulged his grandiose personality and unusual whims."

"So, what's so odd about that?" She smiled, feeling confident in her appearance once again.

"He was mad. A British businessman driven mad by failure of his finances. He did have a strong humanitarian sense of reform and an interest in his public. A colorful figure who died in 1880 and had in attendance at his funeral over thirty thousand citizens of San Francisco."

"How wonderful. He'd be pleased to know that his city is now the financial center of the West, wouldn't he?"

"Who knows?" Watching the waiting group of tourists crowding the wharf, anxious to board the cruise ship after his group disembarked, he smiled indulgently at her rapt face.

"Enjoy our trip?"

"Every single minute." She reached for his hand and, holding it, felt a frisson of emotion at the contact. "Thank you very much."

"Enjoy it more than with your last companion?"

Her brow furrowed as she contemplated his question for a moment before answering. Her mischievous personality enjoyed his look of consternation, but finally she sighed, "Well, that's a hard question. I loved my companion very much."

"The hell you did. Who was he?" he asked, jealous at the thought of her loving another man.

"Not he but she. I took my mother on a brief tour of the city when she stayed with me for a couple of weeks last year."

"You deliberately did that to tease me!" He took her

hand in his, made a path through the crowd, and helped her onto the wharf.

Laughing as her legs grew accustomed to the steady hard walkway beneath her feet, she exclaimed, "No wonder sailors walk with a rolling gait after months at sea."

Hand in hand they strolled through Ghirardelli Square, once a profitable chocolate factory, now refurbished into a fascinating shopping mall. After admiring its unique variety of shops, they wandered slowly back to Fisherman's Wharf.

A tantalizing aroma brought them to a halt in front of an outside café. The pungent smell of steamed crabs was overpowering as they watched the bubbling copper pots.

Derek made his way easily through the crowd to purchase small seafood cocktails topped with zesty sauce. Spooning the delicious crab and shrimp into their mouths, they walked to the edge of the wharf to look at the bobbing boats.

Content, De-Ann inhaled the salty tang of the crisp bay breeze. Mingled with the aroma of seafood, it was an unforgettable scent. Sea gulls screeched as they fought over scraps thrown by the many visitors. The clang of the cable cars could be heard over their cries.

"Let's go take a ride," Derek blurted out, taking her hand and tossing their empty cups and forks into a trash can. His long strides soon carried them to the corner, where they joined the throng waiting to ride the famous cars.

Laughing breathlessly, she clung to him, scolding humorously, "You big brute. I can't keep up with you with your giant strides. You darn near dragged me the entire way!"

"Hang on tight and watch this."

She was amazed to find herself swung into a seat as soon as the noisy car stopped. Derek stood in front of her, hanging on as they clanked up the steep hill, the tiny car bursting to the seams with laughing people. Within moments they had returned down the hill, their place taken by another excited tourist.

Exuberant, his towering body filled with energy, Derek took De-Ann from one attraction to the next along the wharf. Hours later, her feet sore from the walking, she rebelled.

"That's it, you vigorous one-man tour guide. I'm pooped. You can romp around these hills all you want, but I want to sit somewhere nice and quiet and enjoy at least a half hour without moving!"

"Softy. We've been to the wax museum, Ripley's Believe It or Not Museum, looked through all the movie houses, walked through the Maritime State Historical Park and Fort Mason, looked over the boats in the marina, and now you give out."

"Absolutely!" she moaned, stopping to remove an annoying pebble from her shoe. "Not only that, I'm starved. I didn't eat breakfast and you only bought me one little seafood cocktail."

"Okay, I can take a hint, you greedy female. Can you walk or do I have to carry you to my favorite restaurant on the wharf?" Without waiting for an answer, he picked her up in his arms, uncaring of the amused glances of the people staring at him.

Pummeling his back, she leaned to his ear and whispered furiously through gritted teeth, "Put me down this instant. I feel like an idiot!"

"Through complaining that I walk you to death and don't feed you?" he mocked grimly, his hold tight, strides long as he walked forward.

"Yes!"

Stopping, he set her on her feet, his hand remaining on her waist as she giggled helplessly.

"Fool! Are you sure you're not a relative of Emperor Norton?" she taunted. She tucked her blouse back into the waistband of her slacks before smoothing her hair. "Now I'm all mussed up again."

Stopping in front of an elegant restaurant, Derek explained, "We're going to dine at Nick's. He's a friend of mine and owner of a chain of the most fantastic Italian restaurants in the world including most of those I've eaten at in Italy."

Recognized as he entered the plush foyer, Derek smiled at the host, dressed in formal black slacks and vest, his white shirt and tie spotless. "How's it going, Luigi? Get us a good table by the window, please, while we freshen up a bit."

They both returned at the same time, hair combed, hands washed, and hunger pangs gnawing at their stomachs. Luigi led them to the upper floor overlooking the harbor. Sinking into the large booth, De-Ann gave a sigh of pleasure; she surreptitiously eased off her sandals beneath the table.

"Did you take your shoes off?" he questioned, reading her sigh correctly.

Nodding, she smiled without a qualm. "The carpet here is plush and clean and feels oh-so-good to my aching feet."

"Aren't a relative of Emperor Norton, are you?" He laughed as he reached for her hand. Cupping it in his broad palm, he raised it to his lips, placing a lingering kiss below her wrist.

"Why so gallant?" she queried, her stomach clenching as the blood surged through her veins in a burst of pleasure from the touch of his seeking mouth.

"When in Rome, do as the Romans."

"This is only an Italian restaurant," she reminded him, pulling her hand unsuccessfully as he continued to hold it in a tight grip.

"Close enough!" He grinned, sliding around the booth, his taut thighs touching hers as they read the large menu together.

"You decide for me, Derek. The menu's a delight and I'm so starved that anything sounds delicious." Smiling as their handsome young Italian waiter, impeccably dressed in black and white, took their order, she glanced at Derek.

His expression was stern and he glared at her fiercely. "You didn't have to give that obnoxious young gigolo such a come-on look, did you?"

Her laughter was soft as she taunted mischievously. "Well, he is pretty cute. Those big beautiful brown eyes really made my stomach churn."

"Hunger pangs only, minx. Do you want coffee or iced tea?"

"Iced tea sounds wonderful." As their waiter returned she deliberately turned her head to look at the view from their second-story window. When he left, she teased, "Is that better?"

"You're learning. The damn young fool darn near spilled our water looking over your mane of auburn hair and sexy figure straining against your blouse."

"Enough, Derek. You'll make me laugh so hard, I'll spoil my dinner." She started nibbling on the delicious crisp vegetables and slices of salami and cheese on the tray.

"Absolutely great." Derek cut a thick slice of crusty sourdough bread, liberally spread it with butter, and handed it to De-Ann. Thanking him, she smiled with pleasure as they quietly sat, enjoying their delicious plate of antipasto.

"Do you know why the bread here is unexcelled?" she asked.

"No."

"I've heard it's because they bake the fog right into it.

99

Sourdough bread equal to that baked here has been made all over the world but never duplicated. The same ingredients and same recipe don't taste the same as this."

"Whatever it is I agree it's delicious," he remarked, buttering his third slice.

They talked as they enjoyed their leisurely dinner, their rapport complete. De-Ann was amazed by the continued discovery that they agreed on many things; her love for Derek flowered.

Letting her fingers trail over his lean fingers, she turned his palm up. "You have calluses."

"I know. I still work hard, even though I have all the money I'll ever need the rest of my life. I enjoy building. I'm not gifted like you with unique and artistic penmanship. My talents lie in creating beauty from wood, glass, and metal." His eyes locked with hers as he grabbed her hand. "Will you travel with me to see my Hidden Cove home? Once you see it, you'll love it as I do and you'll never want to leave."

Uncertain under what terms he meant, she nodded. "Not tonight, though. I'm too filled with antipasto, minnestrone soup, *scampi ai ferri, cannelloni alla parmigiana,* and spumoni."

"You should be, the way you ate. I hardly got a bite!"

Glaring at him, her eyes shone as she retorted quickly.

"Hardly got a bite? You ate everything I did and a plate of lasagna too."

"I forgot. Okay, we'll call it even, then. Let's go for a long drive before I drop you off at your apartment." After paying the waiter, whose eyes lingered sensuously on De-Ann, he took her arm and escorted her firmly from the room. His possessive hold showed his determination to assert ownership in front of the amorous young man.

Relaxing in the car, the windows open and the soft breeze caressing her face, she sat blissfully, enjoying the sound and feel of the luxurious car as it purred toward Sausalito.

Derek, without any particular destination in mind, eased north, making a wide circle through Richmond, across the Oakland Bay Bridge back into San Francisco.

Checking the time, Derek said he'd better go. At her door he turned to her and extended his arms. De-Ann could feel her heart beat rapidly in anticipation of his kiss. But Derek merely took her in a brotherly hug, then left abruptly.

De-Ann stood on the porch, watching as he walked down the stairs, got into his car, and pulled away without a backward glance.

Stunned by his sudden departure and lack of affection, she stormed into her room. She threw her clothes into the clothes hamper and sank into a tub of warm water filled with the heady essence of her most expensive bubble bath.

Grumbling at Derek's complex personality, she forced his unusual departure from her mind and dreamed of her exciting day. "It will take a sharp woman to capture him," she exclaimed to the silent room. "Someone willing to take the time to delve deeply into his complex behavior. Some-one like me!"

Smug and confident, she scrubbed her soft skin until it glistened. Indulgently she pampered herself with a liberal spray of her most expensive perfume and powder.

Seated in front of the dresser, she brushed her lustrous hair until it glimmered and lay in smooth silky waves over her shoulders. She put on a new robe of jade satin with a deep décolleté neckline and padded barefoot into the kitchen.

Chin raised defiantly, she reached for a bottle of bour-bon and poured a generous portion of the amber liquid over ice in her finest crystal glass. After turning on the radio to an FM station, she curled in a corner of the couch, relaxing like a pampered mistress, a mistress lonesome for her consort.

The soft sounds of a Brahms symphony filled the room, the glorious music adding to De-Ann's wistful frame of mind. Eyes shut, drink untouched on the end table, she rested. Abrupt pounding on the front door roused her from her dreamy state.

The satin of her robe clung to her naked curves as she crossed to the door, the color shimmering in the dimly lit room.

"Who is it?" she asked warily.

"Me!"

Opening the door, she slipped the chain and glared at Derek standing nonchalantly before her. He pushed his way in and kicked the door shut, then reached behind him and latched it before turning to De-Ann.

"Why are you here, Derek Howell?"

"I forgot something."

"What?"

"This." Drawing her unresisting body into his arms, he let the full length of her pliant form mold to his before bending his head. His mouth hovered a brief moment before hungrily taking hers in a kiss so passionate, she was limp and trembling before she could utter a token protest at his arrogant assumption that she would be responsive to his demands.

The dictates of common sense were swept aside by the treacherous response of her body. Her arms clung to the nape of his neck; her lips parted beneath the insistent pressure of his seeking mouth.

Satisfied with her surging response, he slid his hand across her back to her narrow rib cage before moving upward to cup her breast.

Raising his mouth reluctantly from the softness of her lips, he moaned against her neck, "God, De-Ann, why didn't you tell me you were naked beneath this thin piece of cloth?"

"I didn't have time," she whispered, her voice quivering as she wrenched from his hold to walk toward the couch. "You stormed in here and—and assaulted me." Her quick temper rising, she exclaimed, "Why the passion from you now when an hour ago you couldn't wait to leave without a single backward glance!"

"That was your request," he told her without explanation.

"I said nothing to you, Derek. Absolutely nothing!"

"Yes, you did. You told me first thing Saturday morning that you wanted the day to be kept platonic and I did."

"Good heavens, you've got to be kidding. But where have you been this last hour?" she asked, shaking her head in amazement.

"Sitting around the corner listening to one of my eight-tracks on the car stereo. One sixty-minute tape until it was midnight and another day. Did you learn anything from your ridiculous request?"

"Yes! You're completely crazy," she shot back, her eyes dark.

"Were you having a party?"

"No, why?" She followed the direction of his eyes and shrugged. "One drink doesn't make a party. Besides, I didn't touch it anyway."

"Good. I hate women that drink alone."

Her expression mutinous, she walked to the table, intending to swallow the contents of her glass in one gulp.

Aware of her belligerence, he stepped forward, took the glass, and dumped it on a large rubber plant next to the end table. "Now you've got a potted plant in more ways than one." He laughed, setting the empty glass on the table.

"I can't believe you. You are the most opinionated man I've ever met!"

"You are just beginning to find out, my love." Grasping her slender shoulders, he trailed his lips from her forehead to her neck, nibbling along the sensitive cord until he reached her ear.

"You smell so sweet," he murmured huskily. "I want you tonight. I want your lovely body beneath me with my lips caressing each peak and indentation of your delectable figure."

Her cheeks flushed at his harshly spoken request, the low intensity of his voice, and she drew away.

"No, Derek. I want to let you love me but it's too sudden. There's too many responsibilities in such a relationship and I'm just not prepared to—to—"

"Don't say it. It was wishful thinking on my part. I'm not used to denying myself, and you've become a permanent ache in my—"

"Stop, Derek. I'm not that naive!"

"Then I will depart before I take you. My eyes are filled with the image of your naked body on my bed, and now you parade around in that silky garment that clings to your hips and breasts . . . outlines the hardened tips of your nipples."

Turning her back on him, she insisted he leave.

"Good God, don't tell me you're shocked by my honesty? Your breasts are beautiful, and with the tips aroused, even more so." Clasping her shoulder in one hand, he separated the silky hair covering her nape with the other. His mouth seared her tender skin as he placed a delicate kiss on her neck, then he walked abruptly to the door, telling her to be ready at ten that morning for another outing.

Without turning, she heard the door close, then his loud whistle as he walked to his car.

In her room she let the robe slip to the rug. Standing motionless before her full-length mirror, she scrutinized each naked curve of her body. High breasts, rounded in their full maturity, were a perfect ivory background for the rosy peaks of her nipples. Her slender waist curved inward before flaring to rounded feminine hips. Long slender legs were shapely and smooth. A female form ready for its ultimate purpose. Anxious to give of itself to a man and to bear fruit of that giving.

Tearing her eyes from her body, she pulled her nightie over her head and slipped between the sheets for another night alone.

It was hours before she slept, tossing and turning. Hours in which she could contemplate the need of her innermost nature. The restless surging of her heated blood as she ached to explore the delights of her own awakened sensuality tormented her mind, tortured her with indecision of her strict moral beliefs versus the persuasive touch and blatantly honest needs of the man she loved.

CHAPTER SIX

For five weeks Derek courted De-Ann so persistently and tenderly, she was stunned. Even if she was dismayed by his holding back his sensual hunger when he kissed her good night after each evening's entertainment, she was forced to admire his control.

They spent prolonged weekends exploring San Francisco and the surrounding area: places where tourists abounded and those that only the native-born were aware of. Derek, an excellent raconteur, told her stories about each of the places they visited, and De-Ann thrived on them, each of his words stored in her mind.

He held her hand affectionately as they strolled through the zoological gardens. His indulgent smile as she fed peanuts to the elephants and squirrels delighted her tender nature. Always patient, he let her wander to her heart's content.

They took long horseback rides through the miles of bridle paths in Golden Gate Park. He drove her to the viewing area north of Golden Gate Bridge and parked, surprising her with his request to walk back and forth across the long span. The wind blew briskly, dense fog covering the tops of the towers. She was unaware of anything but the enjoyment of his hand on her waist.

De-Ann's love grew by leaps and bounds, her feminine needs blooming with his ardent attentiveness. Hopelessly in love, she felt Derek was only waiting for the proper moment to ask her to be his wife.

Willing to wait, she bode her time, while he continued with his determination to seduce her slowly but certainly. Each night he took her to a different restaurant, those that were formal and cost the earth and those that were small where they wore jeans and T-shirts. They rooted for their favorite world-rated tennis matches at the Cow Palace, screamed for the Giants baseball team at Candlestick Park.

De-Ann's heady whirl continued through a memorable evening at the majestic new Louise M. Davies Symphony Hall where they listened to Maestro Edo de Waart conduct Stravinsky's *Le Sacre du Printemps* in the second-largest performing arts center in the country.

Her mind filled with the glorious sounds, she agreed dreamily to a late-night supper at Nick's restaurant. Derek, dressed in a formal black suit, was so handsome, it took her breath away. His eyes lingered on her gold chiffon gown and the upswept crown of auburn waves. From his expression she knew he was nearing the end of his strict self-imposed emotional control.

She felt the time had finally come to let him know of her love, to tell him she was waiting rapturously, eager to become his wife.

Shown to their former table by the attentive Luigi, they relaxed in the plush comfort of the large booth. Derek leaned forward and placed a tender kiss on the side of her scented cheek. As he was about to speak his eyes caught

107

a figure in the middle of the restaurant. "Well, I'll be damned!" He smiled, standing abruptly.

With curious eyes De-Ann looked up to see a dark, handsome man. He was the same height as Derek, but his features were smoother and his build a fraction lighter. A remarkably handsome man with the same arrogant confidence that she admired in Derek. Beside him stood a tall beautiful woman with glowing violet eyes and long silvery blond hair.

Turning to De-Ann, Derek introduced her to Nick Sandini, the owner of Nick's, and his new bride, Carlyn. He sat beside De-Ann and motioned Nick and Carlyn to sit across from them. He seemed obviously thrilled at meeting his friend, and De-Ann enjoyed listening as they conversed.

Admiring the beauty of Nick's wife, she noticed the deeply contented look in her eyes as they lingered on her husband's face. A look of such blatant love was exchanged when he returned her glance, it was almost embarrassing to witness. Carlyn's face glowed with the pleasure of a woman assured of her husband's undivided devotion.

De-Ann listened to the unbelievable summary of their courtship and recent marriage. The horrifying near-tragedy that Carlyn had experienced during her work as a Los Angeles City police officer caused De-Ann to shudder with sympathy.

Derek turned to De-Ann, holding her hand in a possessive grip. "This handsome friend of mine was one of this city's most eligible bachelors, darling. I was shocked speechless to hear he had swept his bride off to Reno and married without notice."

Looking at Carlyn's striking elegance, Derek complimented her, his husky voice sincere. "You are very beautiful, Carlyn, and appear extremely contented with my friend."

"Thank you, Derek, and you are correct. I've never been happier in my life." She exchanged a tender glance with her husband. Then turning back to Derek, she said, "Nick showed me your outstanding land development, Hidden Coves, on our way south from his mountain home. It looked lovely with many homes much like Nick's."

"Glad you liked it. When did you two return from the deep woods?" he teased, amused as they looked at each other with a secret message of love flowing between them.

"We drove down day before yesterday for the first time since our marriage. We spent the entire summer honeymooning up north. Three months of solitude and heaven," Nick explained. "I stopped in to check with my manager before we fly to Italy for a couple more months of laziness. I want to show off my beautiful bride to my parents and curious relatives."

"Sounds wonderful," De-Ann added wistfully, thinking how fortunate Carlyn was. Nick obviously cherished her, his manner devoted as he unashamedly kissed her palm.

Nick looked apologetically at Derek and De-Ann. "I wish we could join you for dinner but we have to rush. Carlyn's barely had time to look over her new home and we have to leave in the morning on a nine-o'clock flight. Did you know Derek lives only a couple blocks from us, De-Ann?"

"No. I—I haven't been to Derek's home but for a short visit."

"Long enough!" Derek explained confidently, looking mockingly at De-Ann's flushed face.

Kicking him under the table, she felt a sharp pinch on her shoulder as he returned her gesture.

"That sounds interesting," Nick teased, picking up on the look between them. "Derek is now one of the most sought-after bachelors left in this fair city, De-Ann."

"Yes, I've heard." She chuckled. "Not from Derek but from my secretary, who reads all the local gossip and reports it to me."

Admiring the beauty of her vulnerable face and glorious hair, Nick looked at Derek and remarked boldly, "When are you going to get married, my friend?" Smiling at his wife, he added, "I can highly recommend it now."

The sudden stiffening of Derek's back shocked De-Ann. She was surprised to see his brows draw together and a deep frown cross his face. Embarrassed, she lowered her lashes, but not before she had seen the quick shock in Nick's and Carlyn's eyes and their sympathy before they glanced away.

Taking the defensive, Derek exclaimed bluntly in an adamant voice, "I have no intention of ever marrying any woman."

Nick's voice softened as he apologized for his social blunder. "Sorry, but from the way you two looked at each other I naturally assumed you were serious. I'm cognizant of love now that I've experienced it, and yours looked obvious."

"Don't apologize, Nick. You're right. I do love De-Ann, although you rushed my telling her."

Flustered, her hands quivering at his declaration, she sat with head lowered, lashes shadowing her cheeks, until she was in control of her stunned nerves enough to raise her eyes.

Placing his arm around De-Ann's shoulders, Derek bent to place a featherlight kiss on the side of her pale temple, his thumbs caressing her shoulder lovingly.

"Never doubt that I love De-Ann. I told her the first moment I met her that she was my possession and she is. My woman until I take my last breath on this earth."

"Well, then?" Nick asked curiously.

"A piece of paper signed by a judge doesn't make a

marriage nor strengthen love. I saw enough misery between married couples to last me a lifetime."

"But there are many happy marriages too, Derek!" Nick interjected. Carlyn, embarrassed for De-Ann, tried to hush Nick.

"I've yet to see one!" Derek answered grimly. "A wedding is nothing but a bind sanctioned by law that makes it hard to separate when the relationship inevitably goes sour."

Abruptly changing the subject, Nick rose from the booth, taking his wife's hand to assist her from the seat. "The bouillabaisse is excellent tonight. I want you both to be my guest and order anything you like. Sorry, but we do have to leave. We haven't even packed yet." Motioning to his waiter to take their order, Nick smiled at De-Ann and promised to get together when they returned from Italy. They started to leave but were stopped by Derek's voice.

"Let me have your address and I'll see you sooner than that. I fly to Spain in two days' time for six weeks to assist their government with a housing project. We can get together some weekend."

Stunned further by Derek's words, De-Ann sat motionless. Crying inwardly, she wondered if there were any further shocking news she would have to suffer through that evening.

Taking the slip of paper with Nick's address on it, Derek placed it in his billfold before sitting down beside De-Ann. His expression was enigmatic as he watched her, his eyes a deep blue as they narrowed.

"I—I didn't know you were leaving for six weeks, Derek," she stuttered, longing to return their conversation to the affectionate mood prior to meeting Nick and Carlyn.

"That is something else I didn't intend you to know

111

until later tonight. I had planned to take you to my home after dinner, so until then we'll forget I brought it up!"

"Fine with me," she shot back, her quick temper stirred by his sudden mood change. "Maybe you'd rather not eat a late-night supper with me now?"

He turned to face her, an earnest look on his tanned face. Squeezing her shoulder, he said huskily, "Of course I want to eat with you. Don't be mad at me, please?"

"Well, then don't embarrass me. I felt like a fool in front of your friends. They looked as if they thought I'd be brokenhearted when you were so emphatic about not marrying me. For your information I wouldn't have any man on a bet either! I'm perfectly content with my single status also." Her lies tore at her heart, and she clenched her fingers until the nails bit into her palms, praying that she wouldn't break down in front of Derek.

"I didn't mean to cause you discomfort, darling. You heard me tell them both that I love you. That also was premature, since I planned to tell you at my home later tonight." His eyes held hers as his voice lowered seductively. "You should have known by the way I treat you how much I love you, how deeply I care."

"Maybe you do with your kind of love, but apparently we don't love the same, Derek. Mine calls for wedding gowns, marriage licenses, and promises of eternal devotion," she whispered poignantly.

"Sounds good but not practical, as I well know. I was convinced at the age of fourteen that nothing destroys a relationship quicker than a marriage license!"

Interrupted by the waiter, they ordered. The ensuing silence was uncomfortable as they waited for their meal. De-Ann counted the minutes until she could be alone in the privacy of her home, until she could bury her face in her hands and cry her heart out.

The beautifully prepared meal and excellent service

went unnoticed as they made futile attempts to eat their bouillabaisse. The highly seasoned fish stew with its pungent aroma sat in their dishes getting cold. Succulent shrimps, lobster, clams, and seven varieties of fish and spices in a tomato broth could have been sawdust for all the attention it got. Along with the chilled wine, it remained untouched.

"Come on, let's get the hell out of here!" Derek snapped, throwing a large tip on the table and taking her hand firmly.

Following without a word, she entered his car, eager to get to her own apartment. The wheels screeched as he turned sharply onto the main street.

"Take me home, Derek," she pleaded.

"I want to go to my house to straighten this out now," he told her adamantly.

"No. I'm suddenly sick. If you don't get me home in a hurry, I'll pass out on you," she warned, her words suddenly true.

"It wouldn't be the first time, my love," he reminded her.

"Damn it, Derek. I'm not your love, nor am I going to your house tonight," she snapped sharply, her eyes flashing with temper.

Glancing at her white face and the tense clasping of her hands, he decided to comply with her wishes. In the morning they would both be in better control and he could explain his feelings more rationally.

"Okay. We'll talk in the morning when you feel better." Within minutes she was in front of her house. Her hand quivered on the door handle when his sinewy arm reached across and brushed her breasts as he held the door closed.

"No, De-Ann. We can't part like this tonight. I love you and it's tearing my guts apart to feel you withdraw from me. I've caused you pain and you owe it to me to hear my side."

Knowing she was too hurt to talk to him anymore that night, she shook her head no. Her heart pounded with indecision, yet her control was close to breaking. Afraid to speak, she removed his hand.

She opened the door and stepped onto the sidewalk as he sat motionless, shocked by her emphatic refusal to let him explain.

"Good night, Derek. Thank—thank you . . . for everything." The words were barely out when she ran up the stairs and into her apartment. Throwing herself across the spread, she cried. Deep sobs racked her slender body when she was finally able to release the buildup of tensions.

Derek's cynicism to something she thought was the ultimate conclusion of any relationship between two people that loved each other had stunned her to the depths of her soul. Her misjudgment of his intentions had totally destroyed her confidence.

Hours later she rose, tears spent, in control again. Feeling listless, drained of all emotion, she removed her crumpled gown and slipped into jeans, T-shirt, and tennis shoes. Then she packed a nightgown and makeup before pulling on her warm parka. Grabbing her purse, she left her home.

Within minutes of her decision to leave she was in the Mazda, driving as fast as the law allowed to the impersonal sanctuary of a twenty-four-hour motel she knew north of town.

Checked in, dressed in her nightgown, she huddled between the cold sheets. As the clock neared six in the morning she finally slept, the tumbled sheets and damp pillow the only witnesses to the heartbreak that wrenched her slender body during the passing of the long morning hours.

114

She woke shortly before noon and lay listlessly, thinking of everything that had happened. Her independence and temper helped her overcome the sudden rift with Derek. Since he would be leaving San Francisco the next day, she decided to remain in the motel. When she was certain his flight had left, she would return to her job. The resumption of work would help ease the trauma of her unrequited love.

Determined not to mope, she dressed in jeans and T-shirt and walked to the adjoining restaurant. But there she left most of her lunch untouched and finally returned to her impersonal room. Watching television, she counted the hours until Derek would be safely out of the city.

As she thought of their meeting, a vague plan began to form in her mind. Alan's shocking confidence about Derek seeking a surrogate mother for his heir began to torment her. Knowing her love would not dim, De-Ann allowed her bold, tenacious personality to come to the fore. Bravely she decided to gamble everything in an attempt to convince Derek of her continuous devotion.

A grim smile crossed her face as she acknowledged in her heart that what she was doing was wrong. If her plan was successful, the result would be a lifetime of love. If not, she could give that abundant love to their child. Love that she ached to give its father.

Returning to her apartment Monday morning before daylight, she felt as if she had been away a lifetime instead of two long sleepless nights. She showered and dressed in a neat black-and-white-checked two-piece dress. Brushing her hair, she groaned at the way it lay around her face. Filled with electricity, it refused to smooth down despite the vigorous brushing.

Applying her makeup, she smeared her lipstick, then dropped the tube, and as she bent to retrieve it she broke a fingernail.

"Darn, what else can go wrong?" Her exasperated voice rang in the deathly silence of the room.

But when she stuck her finger through her last pair of new panty hose, she began to laugh, the bitter sound bordering on hysteria.

Unfortunately her luck did not change once she left the apartment. She got caught in a traffic jam, was rerouted through an unfamiliar part of the city, and was an hour late for work. Entering her office, she breathed a sigh of relief that she was back in familiar territory and could finally relax.

"Hi, Julie, any mail today?"

The secretary's face lowered and she avoided contact with De-Ann's eyes as she handed her a long manila envelope with the name of her landlord printed in the upper left-hand corner.

"De-Ann, can I talk to you before you read the mail?" Julie asked, her face flushing with embarrassment.

"Sure, what's the matter?"

"I'm pregnant again!" she blurted out, obviously unsure of De-Ann's reaction to the news.

"Congratulations! What's the problem?" she inquired as she opened the large envelope curiously.

"I have to quit within one month. My doctor says I'm carrying this baby differently, and if I want to keep it, I'd better take it easy. He'll let me work for the full month, though, which will give you plenty of time to find a replacement."

Smiling at Julie, she reassured her, "Don't worry, Julie. The most important thing is that you have another nice, beautiful, healthy baby. I'll manage fine."

As Julie went on about the doctor's advice De-Ann hurriedly scanned the letter from her landlord. A legal termination of her lease, effective within thirty days. The building had been sold with a fifteen-day escrow, and all tenants were requested to relocate within one month from the date of the letter.

Stunned by the news, she sat at her desk, speechless, her mind reeling. What was she to do? A sudden inspiration struck her. She called Julie and told her about the lease.

"Call Mr. Percy for me, Julie. I think I'm going to take stock of my life and opt for a complete change."

When he was connected, De-Ann answered brightly, "Mr. Percy, this is De-Ann Wagner. Did you ever find someone to illustrate your children's book?"

Pleased by his news, she smiled, telling him her sudden change of status as a shop owner. "I'm going to buy some property north of town—maybe near Bodega Bay. But anyway I would love to do your book. The reason I said no before was due to the amount of time it would take. If you can give me a month or so to locate a home, I'll be ready to devote full-time to your stories."

She was suddenly pleased with the turn of events. As she told Julie about her plan for buying a small coastal home and working from it instead of an office, excitement filled her in anticipation of the change. She asked her secretary to phone her attorney, Paul Anderson, and see if she could set up an appointment for that afternoon.

She herself phoned a local realtor and told him what she was looking for, then started on the backlog of work. By refusing to accept any new work she would be able to complete everything on hand well within the time before she had to vacate her shop. The amount of work would help take her mind off Derek. By the time he returned from Spain she would be living out of the area. It would be a year before they'd meet again. Most likely close to ten or eleven months until he was wise to her scheme.

Entering the offices of Anderson, Mahan, Jawarski, and Steele sharply at four o'clock, De-Ann looked with admiration at the furnishings, luxuriously decorated with custom-designed tables and chairs, in a burnt umber and brown color scheme. Walls of glass in the twenty-ninth-floor office overlooked the center of downtown.

After giving her name to the main receptionist, she sat on the high-backed chair to wait. A dull throbbing beat across her forehead as the tension regarding the coming meeting tightened her nerves. In a few minutes she was shown into the office of Alan's father and greeted cordially by the intelligent gray-haired man.

Seated in front of his desk, she leaned forward, purse clasped tightly in her lap. With unwavering eyes she looked at his interested face.

"Mr. Anderson, if I ask you something in confidence, will you assure me of your promise not to mention it beyond this office?"

"Certainly, my dear," he told her confidently. "How may I help you?"

"I have been told that a client of yours, Mr. Derek Howell, has solicited your services in hopes of finding a surrogate mother for his child."

Stunned by her knowledge, he sat back, hands clasped beneath his chin. "My son told you, I presume. He is the only one outside myself who knows this information. My own secretary is unaware of the name of my client."

Refusing to acknowledge Alan's reckless words, she shocked the attorney further by saying bluntly, "I want to carry his child."

"Why?"

"The reasons are my own, other than the obvious. I lost my lease and am forced to relocate within thirty days. I want to buy a coastal home and with the price of property I need the money desperately." She lied, knowing she'd never use a single penny.

"But, my dear, you must realize my client will not pay

118

the sum of thirty thousand dollars until he receives his newborn child."

"I know that, but I could arrange my financing to meet those conditions." Her face calm, appearance poised despite the relentless churning in the pit of her stomach and the throbbing across her temples, she inquired, "Have you found a suitable woman yet?"

"No. It is very difficult to discreetly conduct a search for a surrogate mother. One who meets the stringent needs of my client."

"Will—will Mr. Howell be aware of the woman's identity?"

"No. He leaves the final choice to me. To avoid any unforeseen complications from this unique request I felt it best and to both their advantages if they never know who the other is."

"I agree, but unfortunately I already know who Mr. Howell is. I feel I would be ideal, sir. I'm healthy, fully mature, have a strong, intelligent background, am a responsible adult and mentally stable enough to act in an unemotional manner."

"You would be ideal, my dear. More than ideal, as you are also extremely beautiful, but I regret that I must say no." His eyes scrutinized the sudden paling of her face at his answer and he frowned.

"In addition to your beauty," he continued, his voice drumming through her mind, "you appear vulnerable. I need a woman with a streak of mercenary blood in her, one who could abandon her newborn child without a thought of remorse after she received the fee for delivery."

"A woman wouldn't have to be mercenary or necessarily uncaring, I don't think. It could be that she would be filled with an overabundance of love instead, would receive her pleasure from making Mr. Howell happy and knowing her child would never want for a single thing throughout his life."

"I never looked at it from that angle, De-Ann," he answered quietly, his brows drawing together as he pondered her soft-spoken words.

"Many children are raised by one parent. This child would be no different. Plus he would have the advantage of a strong, intelligent male influence on his life."

"Are you willing to sign legal contracts? Could you walk away from the hospital without the child in your arms?"

"Yes," she answered, her eyes direct as she swallowed back the feeling of remorse over her lie.

"Would you be willing to follow the advice of the physicians that will impregnate you artificially?"

A slight flush staining her cheeks, she nodded. "Of course, without that process there would be no question of my seeking to bear his child."

He paced in back of his desk before stopping to look at her for a long moment. "Let me think about it. Frankly I'm stunned by your request, although I must admit you are what I have been unsuccessfully seeking."

Stepping forward, he took her hand as she stood, his eyes penetrating hers deeply, their keen insight questioning her motives silently.

"Let me call you in a few days. I have to be extremely cautious, as you must realize. The far-reaching repercussions could be disastrous for all three of you."

"Three?"

"Yes, my dear. You, my client, and the child."

"Of course, I was forgetting. Thank you, Mr. Anderson. I'll be looking forward to your phone call."

"Any time, my dear. Ah, but I wish my weak, ineffectual son would mature enough to attract a lovely, independent woman such as you," he told her bluntly. The smile

120

that lighted her face, the beauty of her hair and eyes, caused him a sudden yearning for his past youth.

"Alan will be fine, Mr. Anderson. Give him a few more years and he'll make you very proud."

"Thank you, my dear. I certainly hope so."

Leaving his office, she knew she had planted the seeds for her request. Hopefully they would mature and he would see her as the ideal woman for the carrying of his client's heir. She knew she was attempting the most deceitful thing she would ever do in her life, but she felt the rewards would be worth the lies.

After parking the car in the garage, she walked to her door. Head down, exhausted by the lack of sleep in the motel, she entered her apartment.

Immediately sensing Derek's presence with the built-in sensitivity that flowed between them, she stopped. Her glance around the room found it empty.

"Derek?" her soft voice rang out nervously.

"Yes, my love," he answered, walking blithely from her kitchen.

Face white with shock, she cried out, "But you're supposed to be in Spain."

"I know, and according to everyone, I am. I couldn't leave until we talked. You refused to let me explain how I felt Saturday, and fled your home like a war refugee. It's your fault that I'm not taking care of my important commitments now."

Her green eyes widened, the hurt vulnerability showing in their depths, and she faced him. "Why—why are you tormenting me?"

"Tormenting you? My God, I don't think I've slept since you were with me last. Sit down!" he ordered, walking toward her, his eyes narrowed and ruthless. "You're going to listen to my reasons for saying what I did to Nick and then we can make plans after that."

"All right, Derek. I'll listen to you, but your emphatic statement still rankles, so don't be surprised if I show you the door as soon as you've finished with what you have to say."

"Fair enough." Sitting across from her, hands clasped between his knees, he leaned forward.

"I intended to take you to my home after our meal at Nick's," he began.

"Why?"

"I wanted to ask you to be my mistress. The trip to Spain was to be our honeymoon."

"Honeymoon! Without a marriage is there even such a thing?" she blurted out, her hands nervously raised as she curled up in the corner of her couch. Feeling defenseless in his presence, she swallowed the pain in her throat at his words.

"Don't interrupt. I said we would always be honest with each other and I meant it. To be perfectly candid, I had also planned to seduce you. The past few weeks had become unbearable to me. I was finding it increasingly difficult to control myself around you. I wanted you, De-Ann, and I knew you wanted me equally. I thought my timing was correct and that you were ready to come to me that night." He huskily added, "My libido couldn't abide a casual visit."

The color left her face completely and she shook her head, hoping to stop his words, aware now why he'd kept her from his home.

"Was—was that all I ever was to you? A quick lay then good-bye?"

"Of course not. I told you I loved you. I always will love you but I can't marry you. I couldn't bear it if you left me after we were man and wife. The pain of your loss would be more than I could stand."

"But what makes you think I'd leave you?"

"Every example I've seen of marriage has added to my cynicism of it. I hope you don't think I'm telling you this with conceit, but I must make you understand if we are to have a life together."

"All right, Derek, I'll listen," she agreed solemnly, her eyes never leaving the nervous tremors of his face muscles nor the tautness of his clenched hands.

"My first memories of my beautiful mother were of her making love to a man in the library of our home. Unaware what was happening, I blundered into the room to talk with her and my father. The man was not my father, but one of a series of lovers that entertained her during the day. At night she was a loving wife, and my father never knew of her duplicity until she abruptly left with one of her wealthier men friends."

She shook her head with sympathy for the young boy's unhappy childhood, so different from her own. Yet she remained silent, letting him vent his anger and early frustrations.

"My father changed completely after this. He started drinking and began to run around also. I was raised by a series of cold, unemotional housekeepers who felt put upon to have the added responsibility of a child thrust on them.

"My father was handsome and wealthy. The women flocked to him. When I was fourteen, he married a woman younger than him who seemed totally devoted to his happiness. I was pleased when they got married as I figured he would quit drinking and I was anxious to lead a more normal life."

"What happened, Derek?"

"The night they returned from their honeymoon the bitch came to my room. Hell, I was just a damn kid. Still interested in sports and youthful amusements, though I was big and fairly mature-looking. She crawled into my

123

bed as I slept. Her voluptuous naked figure laying over me woke me up. Her eager hands groped for my body as she told me my dad had drunk himself into a stupor and couldn't do her any good.

"It was horrible. She damn near scared me to death. The upshot was my father found out about it and never trusted me after that day. His other wives were even worse, but I won't go into that. I was mature enough by then to avoid their invitations. I lied about my age, joined the Marines for four years, and straightened out my mind enough to pursue my own interests. By then I was mature enough to want a woman to satisfy my own needs and soon learned how to please them too."

"Don't, Derek. Please, I . . . don't want to hear any more now," she cried out, her body racked with jealousy.

"Yes! Hear me through to the end. I insist on it. I became a taker. A taker anytime I had the need because I found the world full of women seeking the same thing I was. Mercenary women willing to sell their bodies for a smile, an expensive gift, or a satisfying romp in the sack."

"God, you were horrible too!" she retorted, appalled by his tale.

"Probably, but I never resorted to seducing virgins until I met you. The moment I saw you I knew I had to have you and planned to take you that first night. Can you imagine my chagrin when you woke untouched the next morning in my bed to tell me you'd never slept with a man!"

"But I haven't."

"I know. This added to the complications of my life. I knew I had to have you, yet my conscience bothered me for the first time. Shrugging it aside, I became determined to seduce you. By then I was so in love with you, I didn't care how I managed it as long as you ended up as my mistress."

"Oh . . . Derek. You're so cynical, I can't believe it. Didn't you ever meet any nice women?"

"Not in my circles, darling. Every woman I've met young enough to be interested in sex has approached me at one time or another. Many I have taken but never one that was married. I have never made love to a woman married and living with her husband. If one attracted me, it was only a matter of time until she was divorced and I could have her."

Standing up, she cried out with pain, "I can't stand it. Derek, please don't say any more." Her hands covered her face and she wept. Wept for the young boy influenced by his unfaithful mother. Cried for the youth rejected by his father. But mostly sobbed over the thought that he might never change, that his deep mistrust of a faithful, loving relationship had ruined the blossoming of their deep love.

Coming to her, he clasped her shoulders and pulled her harshly into his arms. Hands clasping her face, he raised it to him.

"Come to me, De-Ann. Be my mistress. I love you and I'll protect you with my life."

"Your life but not your name," she blurted out, her eyes shimmering with unshed tears.

"I told you why. I couldn't live if I found you were unfaithful to me."

"I could be unfaithful despite not being married," she explained resentfully.

"I would see that you weren't. It's never the same."

"What about children? Would you see I didn't get pregnant too?" she retorted, her face held firmly in his grip.

"Naturally. I need an heir only to pass on my name and fortune. You would be my mistress, my love. My child has been arranged for. His or her appearance will not affect our life."

"What? You're crazy!"

"Maybe, but only about you." His head lowered and his mouth parted to take her lips, but she wrenched to get away.

"Stop!" Clamping his lips over her mouth, he enfolded her trembling body, forcing her to respond as he relentlessly held her still. He trailed kisses along the smooth skin of her neck, his voice muffled as he moaned, "I love you, De-Ann. Come to me, my darling. Let me have you now."

Pulling from the punishing hold of his strong arms, she leaned back, shaking her head no as tears slid unchecked down her cheeks. But Derek ignored her silent answer and caressed the hollow of her exposed vulnerable throat, his lips searing the rapidly beating pulse in a hot torturous kiss.

"No . . . no . . ." she groaned as his lips left her throat to trail downward to the cleavage between her breasts.

His deft fingers unbuttoned her blouse, cupped her firm breast as he pulled down the skimpy low-cut edge of her bra. "Oh, God, you're beautiful," he muttered brokenly before his mouth took the soft pink point into his mouth in a worshiping caress that rocked her nerves to the tips of her toes.

Her hands crept around his neck, fingers clutching the thick hair on his nape. The touch of his tongue circling the hardened tip of her breast before his mouth trailed kisses over the silky texture caused her legs to buckle.

Holding her limp form to him, he pulled her to the couch. He lowered his body over hers, intent on possessing every delectable, trembling inch. Placing his taut thigh between her legs, he reached for her blouse to remove it.

"Now, my darling. Now I will show you how much I care."

His voice broke into her subconscious, rousing De-Ann from his mesmerism. She slapped at him sharply, at the same time slipping out from beneath his body. Breasts heaving, visible in the opening of her blouse, she faced him.

"Get out, Derek! Get out of my apartment. You don't love me. You only want me as your mistress. That's not enough!"

Slender chin raised proudly, eyes darkened to jade, she forced herself to reject him, despite the relentless pounding of her heart. Knowing she was taking a horrendous chance, she prayed. If they were ever to have any chance at happiness, she would have to turn him from her.

Standing her ground, she told him truthfully, "I love you, Derek. You also know I want you, but I refuse to be used."

"Not used, my darling, but loved," he moaned, standing by the door. His narrowed eyes scrutinized her lovely face, feeling the fiery dignified determination flow between them. "I could have taken you now," he told her calmly.

"I know that, Derek. I also know I would have given myself to you with all the love in my heart if you had. But that's not enough for me. I need all of you. Your name as well as the portion of your heart you're now willing to share."

Turning her back, she told him to leave. The sound of his hand on the knob as he opened the door tore through her body. Small hands tightly clenched, she remained adamant.

"I will come to you as your wife, Derek, or not at all!"

His footsteps rang through her mind like a death sentence as he left her, the closing of the door having barely made a sound.

A black wave crossed over her eyes and shivering uncontrollably, she tried desperately to regain her equilibrium. As she rushed to call him back, to plead with him to stay under any conditions, she tripped.

She lay stunned by his departure, a tiny dejected figure on the living room floor. Disillusioned, her mind ached with the torment of the man she loved leaving without a backward glance.

CHAPTER SEVEN

Late afternoon the following Friday De-Ann returned from a bank appointment to find her secretary filled with anxiety.

"Julie, what's the matter?" she inquired softly before the door had a chance to jangle closed behind her.

"Mr. Howell phoned from Spain. He seemed so upset you weren't here that I didn't know what to say. He said he would call you at your apartment tonight at seven."

Heart pounding at the sound of his name, she felt her hands start to tremble. In her office she sat at the desk, her legs trembling too much to stand.

Oh, Lord, she thought silently, *will it always be like this? Will I always shake at the sound of his name? Will the sight of every dark man with a powerful build and arrogant stance cause me to tremble?*

Her secretary's face peering with concern around the office wall brought a smile to her lips.

"I'm fine, Julie. It's just that there have been so many things happening this week. I've been working until two every morning to complete my assignments before the end of the lease. I guess I'm overly tired."

"Did—did you and Mr. Howell have an argument?" Julie asked bravely. "You never mention his name anymore, De-Ann."

"A fight with Derek? Good heavens, no. He's in Spain working for the next couple of months. Of course we can't see each other until he returns." Smiling, she lied with compunction.

"Gosh, the way he rushed you the last few weeks I should think you both need a rest. He took you out each evening, phoned once or twice a day." Her plain face shining with romantic thoughts about Derek and De-Ann, she sighed wistfully. "I thought you would have been married by now. He sent flowers, gave you gifts, and courted you like the hero in my last paperback. It was—He's so handsome! I think I'd swoon if he looked at me like I've seen him stare at you."

Her bitter laughter sounded shrill as she scorned her secretary's infatuation with Derek. "Women don't swoon anymore, Julie. Nor do all men have marriage in mind, for that matter," she added as an afterthought.

Wanting to change the subject from Derek, she questioned her secretary further about any phone calls.

"Oh, I almost forgot. Mr. Anderson wants you to come to his office at five tonight. Sorry, De-Ann, but it completely slipped my mind after talking with Mr. Howell."

She checked her watch. "Good, that gives me an hour and a half to complete these invitations." Soon after dismissing Julie, she was involved with her impeccable printing on the last of four hundred hand-lettered wedding invitations for a young debutante from Hillsborough, a tedious job that had taken every minute of her working time since Tuesday morning. She was proud of her originality in the artistic design that bordered the envelopes and announcements, and had received enthusiastic praise from the affluent parents of the bride.

Breathing a sigh of relief, she finished the last name. Eager to see her attorney, she made quick work of cleaning up her supplies, the invitations neatly stacked in their boxes, waiting to be picked up the following Monday.

Fresh makeup applied, hands washed, hair smoothly brushed, she was ready to drive to his office. Her stomach churning, she wondered what his final decision would be. She was willing to fight for the right to bear Derek's child. Without his son or daughter burgeoning in her womb, she was afraid he would suppress his avowed love for her in the willing arms of another woman.

Arriving several minutes early, she was dismayed to see Alan leaving his father's office. She sat in the corner of the main reception area with her head turned in hopes he wouldn't spot her, but she was unfortunate.

His long strides carried him to her side until he stopped before her, hands on hips. His voice was loud in the empty office.

"Surprised to see you here, De-Ann. May I ask why?"

It was impossible not to compare his handsome, yet pampered, face with the strength of Derek's features. Alan lacked soundness of character, as well as the overpowering vigor of Derek's muscular body.

"You may not, Alan!" she retorted sharply.

"Still mad at me?" he asked, his expression stubborn, mouth petulant and soft.

"Yes!"

"Because I got too drunk to drive you home?"

"No, because you didn't believe me when I said I had not slept with Derek Howell."

"So I was a few days premature. What's the difference what week it was? I read the papers and talk with friends of his. Rumor has it that you two have been inseparable for the past couple months."

"That doesn't mean we spent the entire time in his bed!" she retorted, her temper beginning to flare at his attitude and moral smugness, despite his own efforts along that line.

"Maybe not the entire time, but there's not a soul who wouldn't believe most of it wasn't spent there. The big man's not known for his monklike leanings and you're a beautiful woman."

"You're all wrong if you think he touched me. You more than anyone should know I won't be coerced into any man's bed without a marriage license." Holding her left hand up to him, she told him angrily, "As you can see, I have no ring on my finger."

His bitter laugh taunted her. "Well, if that's the case, my dear, then you'll be the only one he doesn't score with. No woman will get his band of gold. The man's emphatic in his desire to stay single. Are you forgetting what I told you that night?"

"About his wanting a surrogate mother for his heir rather than give up his life-style?"

"That's it. After the rush he gave you, if you really didn't put out, then you can kiss his attentions good-bye. From what I hear, he's in Spain now and you know how lovely those dark-haired senoritas with their beautiful dark brown eyes are."

"I agree, Alan. Many of the women are exceedingly gorgeous," she said softly, refusing to let his jealous taunts destroy her composure.

Despite the last few months, Alan still felt compelled to seek De-Ann's company. Her refusal to date him anymore had caused him many sleepless nights. Nights when he was aware she was in Derek's company and his vivid imagination, picturing them making love, tormented him relentlessly. His envy of Derek had left him bitter.

"Will you have dinner with me, De-Ann?" he pleaded meekly.

She shook her head before telling him no. "Sorry, Alan, I've got many things on my mind at the moment and dating is out for a while. Thanks anyway."

Called into the office by the young receptionist, who smiled invitingly at her boss's son, she bid Alan good-bye. He was not at all in her thoughts as she entered his father's office.

Once seated, she asked without preamble, "Did you come to a decision, Mr. Anderson?"

"Yes, but it's against my instincts." He watched De-Ann through narrowed eyes for several moments. "I preferred a woman who had already had one child. She would be familiar with impregnation, the months of pregnancy, and childbirth, plus the possible effects of postpartum blues."

Leaning forward and folding his hands on his desk, he went on after a tension-filled pause. "I have decided to concede to your wishes, my dear. I'm certain you will have a beautiful, healthy baby for my client."

Color tinged De-Ann's cheeks at his remark. She found it difficult to maintain her poise. Only when he handed her several sheets of a legal contract to read did her mind clear. She leaned back in her chair, reading each word carefully.

"I'll sign it. When can arrangements be made with the clinic?"

"As soon as my client returns from his overseas trip. Until I had located a suitable surrogate mother, there was no need for him to be a donor."

"Yes, of course, I can understand that." As she reached

into her purse for a pen to sign the documents, he stopped her, his expression concerned.

"Wait a moment, my dear. Are you absolutely certain this is a wise choice? What about your friends? The interference with your job? Your own mother and relatives?" His keen eyes studied her. "The conceivable mental complications after delivery?"

"I thought very carefully of all this before I contacted you." Her eyes lowering, she clasped her handbag before looking him in the face. Voice steady and soft, she continued.

"No one will know about my being pregnant. I've lost my lease to my shop and intend to purchase a small home north of the city in a lovely bayfront town. I'm going to tell my friends that I'm leaving the country for several months to study."

"But what about your mother? She'll have to know."

"Of course. I'll explain everything to her and she'll understand. No one but my mother will know what I'm doing."

"Your mother and your own vulnerable conscience."

Startled by his wording, she looked up to see him staring thoughtfully at her, his poor choice of words unintentional.

"I'll be fine."

"I think you just might be right, De-Ann. You have an unusual ability to convince someone you're doing the right thing," the lawyer said, watching her sign the agreement.

She was relieved to see that nowhere had the wording been such that she was breaking any laws with her future intentions. The contract appeared more binding on the mother's rights for full medical support and payment on delivery of his child than it did on the surrogate mother's obligation to actually turn over the child to the father after birth.

134

Perfect, she thought to herself as she handed the papers to Alan's father. *So far everything has gone better than I had hoped.*

De-Ann was given the final details regarding a physical examination by a prominent local gynecologist. She agreed to wait for Mr. Anderson's call about the actual procedure of artificial insemination. These instructions clear, she left her attorney's office hurriedly, unaware of Alan watching curiously from the end of the long hall.

The phone was ringing as she unlocked her front door. Throwing her purse down on the nearest chair, she answered breathlessly.

"De-Ann?" His deep voice coming across the thousands of miles that separated them still had the power to cause her legs to buckle. Hands clasping the receiver in a tight grip, she sat on the couch to steady herself.

"Y-yes. Hello, Derek."

"Apparently your secretary told you I would phone tonight?"

"Yes, but she didn't tell me your reasons," she whispered, her voice barely audible with the constriction in her throat.

"I wasn't about to tell her I sent you an airplane ticket to fly to me." He paused then, and De-Ann could hear the anxiety in his voice when he continued. "I need you, De-Ann. Come to me soon."

"As your mistress, you mean?" she queried, her forehead beaded with perspiration as she felt suddenly faint.

"As my lover, darling. It's tearing me apart to be away from you. I've rented a large estate just for the two of us."

Hurt by his continued cynicism toward marriage, she stormed at him in a sudden temper.

"I hope you didn't pay more for one with a double bed."

"Why, De-Ann?"

"Because you won't need the extra width to sleep with me!"

She slammed down the receiver in a rage. The sound of his pleading question brought back all the memories of their happiness, plus the despair of their misunderstanding. She walked to her room, but her hands were shaking so badly, she found it hard to undress. Listless, she slipped into her robe, Derek's absence causing a void that seemed to be growing each minute they were apart.

She suddenly felt she needed the comfort of her mother's calm voice and reassurance of her love. Curled in the corner of the couch, she dialed her number, feeling better the instant she heard the cheery greeting.

They talked for several minutes, exchanging news of events that had occurred since their last conversation, until De-Ann began to tell her the reason for her call.

"You better be sitting down, Mom, as I have something to tell you that might be a shock until you understand the full story."

"What is it, dear?" her mother inquired curiously.

"I'm going to have a baby in ten or eleven months."

Her mother's voice rose with excitement as she cooed, "That's nice, dear. When are you getting married?"

"That's the part you might need assurances about. I'm not." Her voice softening, she whispered. "I'm ready for a child but not a husband."

"I don't like the idea of your having sex without marriage, De-Ann," she scolded. "Besides, you know how your father felt about promiscuous behavior."

"But that's what's so great, Mom. I'm not going to have sex!"

"You're twenty-six years old now and well aware of the biological necessities for pregnancy."

Laughing at her mother's ridiculous statement, she

teased mischievously, "I should after all the dire warnings I got at the age of eleven from both of you."

"Apparently they weren't enough!" she retorted.

"Hush, Mom, and listen. I'm going to go to a gynecologist for artificial insemination. I—I have the donor already picked out and it—er—everything will be completed in a totally clinical atmosphere."

"Well, you'll certainly be missing the best part of becoming a parent."

"Why, Mom, shame on you!" She laughed impudently, amazed by her mother's outspoken words.

The older woman's voice suddenly became serious as she chastised her daughter repeatedly. "I think you're very foolish, De-Ann. The entire idea is totally preposterous." Almost as an afterthought she complained, "What could I tell my neighbors when my daughter shows up with my first grandchild and no son-in-law?"

"It would be none of their business!" De-Ann shot back frankly. "I'm well established, my business is prospering more each year, I have an adequate savings account, new car, colorful wardrobe, and nice apartment. I don't need anything else except—"

"A husband!" her mother interrupted, obviously upset.

"That is also a long-range plan. Unfortunately the cart must come before the horse in this circumstance."

"I don't like it, De-Ann. It's totally foolish to have a child without a husband in the first place, then to have one only to turn it over to a baby-sitter while you work makes it selfish too!"

"But, Mom, you don't understand. I have so much love to give."

"Well, then give all that love to a man! Let him give you a baby in the normal way. Each child is entitled to both parents."

"I agree, but there are lots of single parents who

137

through no choice of their own raise babies without a partner."

"Why don't you adopt a child, then?"

"It wouldn't be the same. I—I want to nurture it, carry it in my body, and nurse it at my breast."

"You sound like one of my old banty hens when she became broody, De-Ann, and I'm appalled at you. Now you go take two aspirin, fix yourself a nice meal, and get a good night's sleep."

"I'm not sick, Mom," De-Ann sighed exasperatedly.

"Yes, you are. I don't want to hear another word until you straighten out your mind about this. When you can call and tell me that I have a son-in-law, then I will listen to your plans for having a baby!"

"But, Mom—" she wailed before being interrupted.

"If you don't get over this depressive mood in a month or so, I suggest you take a long vacation. It's obvious that you're overworked and under a severe mental strain."

Changing the subject, De-Ann talked with her mother for several minutes before hanging up the phone. She hadn't really expected her mother to condone the pregnancy, but she was disappointed anyway. Unthinkingly she went to the medicine chest and took down the bottle of aspirin. When she realized her automatic action, she returned the bottle.

Over the weekend as she drove north with a local realtor she was further disappointed to find that property in livable condition was scarce and way beyond her financial means. Coastal homes were limited, but her agent agreed to check with other offices through multiple-listing services. His advice had been discouraging.

Time on her lease running out, De-Ann checked the calendar the following Friday. As she drew a line through the date she saw with alarm how soon she would have to leave her office. Julie was beginning to slacken off with her work and had been late several days with morning sickness, adding to De-Ann's dilemmas.

De-Ann, sympathetic to the younger girl's distress, gave her an extra month's pay and told her to stay home. Knowing she could manage the office work after the shop was closed at night, De-Ann straightened her shoulders, determined to manage efficiently despite her numerous unexpected problems.

Later as she talked with her attorney he explained that his client was pleased that he had found a suitable surrogate mother but was too busy to leave Spain until his contract ran out. That would be at least another month.

The silence of the office without her secretary grated on De-Ann's nerves but she kept working. Long diligent hours were rapidly completing her backlog of jobs.

On Friday of the following week De-Ann looked up as the front door bell jangled. A pleased smile on her face, she greeted Julie, who stood in the office with her two young children—a little girl of three holding her mother's skirt shyly as she looked around the room, and a nine-month-old baby boy in her arm sleeping peacefully.

De-Ann reached for the baby and cuddled his soft little body in her arms, a sudden surge of desire to have Derek's child tearing her heart with sadness. Inhaling his sweet powdery scent, she walked to her office and sat down to rock him in her arms.

Talking to Julie's little girl, who was losing her shyness and beginning to explore, she looked at her ex-secretary.

"What brings you by today, Julie?"

"I was hoping to be the first to congratulate you and Mr. Howell. I—I wish you had told me about it first, though, since I was in on the romance from the start. You never gave me the slightest hint of your plans while I was still working."

De-Ann waited silently for Julie's explanation so she

could find out what she was talking about. Dark lashes hiding the quandary in her eyes, she watched the contented face of the baby boy clasped lovingly in her arms.

"That—that's nice of you, Julie," she murmured softly when the silence between them began to grow uncomfortable.

"Where did you . . . hear about it?" she questioned, wondering what on earth Julie was babbling so excitedly about.

Julie reached into the side pocket of her large carrier bag, which was crammed with clean diapers and bottles, and withdrew a local tabloid. Containing the latest gossip and newsworthy happenings of San Francisco's large group of sophisticates and socially prominent, it had never been of interest to De-Ann.

Taking her baby from De-Ann's arms, Julie watched as she scanned the paper. De-Ann's face paled as she stared at the shocking headlines. The bold print was directly over a picture of her and Derek smiling at each other as they left the symphony hall on their last date. A faint moan escaped her lips as she read the blatant story.

DEREK HOWELL TO MARRY SENSUOUS
SURROGATE

Confirmed this morning, another of San Francisco's eligible bachelors will wed.

Derek Howell, prominent land developer and world-renowned building consultant who was much sought after by this city's elite, has decided to take a bride.

Last of the socially prominent Howell family, early settlers of San Francisco's Nob Hill district, Derek has previously managed to elude the bonds of matrimony.

Mystery surrounds his sudden change of life-style.

Giving up his freedom to marry the woman who had unbeknownst signed a contract with the offices of attorneys Anderson, Mahan, Jawarski, and Steele to be surrogate mother for his heir smacks of intrigue.

When interviewed by this reporter, Derek, whose past aversion to permanent ties has broken many hearts, claims, "It was love at first sight. My lovely fiancée and I will wed before the end of the month and hopefully within the year announce the birth of our first child—conceived in the normal manner, of course!"

Sorry, girls, the stunning auburn-haired beauty Ms. De-Ann Wagner, owner of De-Ann's, is a uniquely talented calligrapher and seems to have penned her man with permanent ink!

"I'm really happy for both of you," Julie blurted out wistfully. "That part about a surrogate mother puzzles me though, De-Ann. That surely wasn't the reason you went to the attorney's, was it? The thought of Mr. Howell ever needing to hire a woman to have his child is too ridiculous to believe. Why, he's an absolute dream."

"Yes, I agree he is a dream, Julie," she answered, ignoring her first question deliberately. "I'm sorry that I have to cut our visit short but I have an appointment across town and I'm late."

Rushing Julie and her children out the door, and promising to keep in touch, she wished them a hasty good-bye. She bolted her office door, uncaring of her lie.

Shades drawn, the CLOSED sign propped in the front window, De-Ann slumped in her office chair. Forehead clasped in her trembling hands, she was filled with indecision.

She sat stunned, unable to comprehend the reasoning behind Derek's shocking announcement to a gossip columnist. Further troubled by her attorney breaking his promise to keep her identity confidential, she shuddered in confusion. The entire matter was becoming more puzzling by the minute as she tried to unravel the motives for Derek's sudden about-face.

Oh, God, she cried inwardly. *All my deceptiveness in agreeing to be surrogate mother to his heir was unnecessary. My betrayal won't even be essential now that he wants to marry me.*

De-Ann gathered her purse, suddenly anxious to get to her apartment in case of a phone call from Spain. With nervous fingers she quickly placed her worktable in order before leaving without a backward glance as the door slammed shut behind her.

As she maneuvered the Mazda through the heavy traffic, she gritted her teeth to keep from yelling out her wrath at the slow drivers in front of her. Fighting the flow of cars, she hit every signal red light, which added to the tension.

By the time her car was parked in the small garage, a raging headache pounded her temples relentlessly. She heard the phone ring twice before she was able to unlock the front door. Heart pounding, she lifted the receiver, praying fervently it was Derek.

CHAPTER EIGHT

The front door slammed shut behind De-Ann. Unnoticed, her purse fell to the rug. With a hesitant voice she started to speak.

"It's time we had a long talk," her mother scolded firmly, interrupting De-Ann's greeting.

"What about, Mom?" she questioned wearily. Disappointment that it wasn't Derek caused her stomach muscles to clench in pain. She slumped dejectedly against the corner of the couch and listened.

"For starters you can explain about the shocking news story I received anonymously in this morning's mail."

"Don't tell me you received a scandal sheet too! I was hoping the news wouldn't reach beyond the San Francisco area."

"Apparently you're aware of the surprising message, then?" her mother asked sharply, dismayed by her daughter's recent behavior.

"Yes, I've read it. Until I talk with Derek, I won't know anymore than you do," she said weakly, hoping for sympathy.

"I can't understand you, De-Ann. A week ago you astound me with the news you've decided to conceive my first grandchild in the sterile atmosphere of a clinic. Today I receive a newspaper announcement that you'll marry within the month. To a man who hired you to act as surrogate mother for his child! Were you intending to keep this baby before he graciously decided to marry you?"

"Yes and no." De-Ann said evasively in a rising voice as she attempted unsuccessfully to make her mother understand. "It's rather complicated. I agreed to be surrogate mother, as the article says, but—but I was"—sobs catching in her throat, she tried desperately to keep control as she expounded her deceitfulness—"I wasn't going to give up my baby. I was going to—to keep it."

"According to the paper, you signed a contract to act as surrogate mother. You were legally bound to give up this child."

"There is no law that can actually force a mother to give up her child despite a written agreement to do so prior to its birth," De-Ann retorted, wiping tears from her flushed cheeks.

"I'm ashamed of you, honey. You've never done anything dishonest in your life until now." Her mother's disappointment was obvious as she chastised De-Ann firmly.

"I—I know, Mom, and I feel sick about it," she cried out, trying to make her understand the reasons behind her treachery.

"I like this man's looks. They show strength. Who is he?"

"I met him several weeks ago. We've dated constantly ever since. I thought he was going to ask me to be his wife." Her voice broke as she sobbed. "He only wanted me as his mistress."

"That doesn't excuse your actions, De-Ann. What did you think you would accomplish?"

"I hoped he would want to marry me when he found out I was the surrogate mother. If—if not, I was going to run off with our baby and raise it by myself."

Scolded by her mother, De-Ann felt her spirits plunge. The throbbing ache in her temples became unbearable.

"Don't scold me, Mom, please. I've had a terrible time the last couple weeks. My whole world appears to have fallen apart, and I've got a beastly headache besides. I've felt wretched since I first thought of the scheme to betray Derek and his attorney, who is a friend of mine."

Tears slipping unheeded down her face, she cried. "I thought I could change his cynicism. When I found I meant no more in the end than his other women, I vowed to do anything that would make him want to marry me!"

"You're an adult now, De-Ann, and responsible for your own mistakes. I love you, honey, though I feel you are in for some troubled weeks ahead. A man under pressure is liable to do things he later regrets. If this happens, you'll be as guilty as he."

Her mother's assurances of love helped ease the sudden shame over her attempts to deceive Derek. Hanging up the receiver after agreeing to keep in touch, she sat motionless.

Trembling fingers rubbed lightly over her eyes, trying to ease the tension. Suddenly a frisson of fear ran across the sensitive nape of her neck and she turned. Blood rushed from her face with the shock of Derek's unexpected appearance.

As he leaned nonchalantly against the kitchen door, a smug expression on his face, it was evident he had heard every word. Wearing a tan business suit with dark brown shirt and patterned silk tie, his broad muscular frame filled the doorway. Deep blue eyes narrowed in contemplation;

the dark shadows beneath them and the hollows in his taut cheeks attested to his stress during the preceding weeks.

De-Ann rose, legs threatening to give way, hands clutched across her breast.

"How—how did you get in, Derek?" she whispered with amazement.

"With the same key I used the last time. I had one made weeks ago from your key ring." His deep voice thundering through the room, he added grimly, "It's a damn good thing too! I overheard every word of your despicable scheme!"

De-Ann's volatile temper gave her the surge of strength she needed to stand up to Derek and she stormed furiously.

"My despicable scheme? What about your blatant announcement in the local newspaper that you were going to marry me? After embarrassing me in front of Nick and Carlyn, now you make an about-face and tell the whole city we're going to wed before the end of the month and have a—a baby within a year!"

"My scheme?"

"Yes! You gave the article. The reporter said you talked with him," she shot back, ired by his accusations.

Derek stood there, rubbing his knuckles with satisfaction, his mouth lifted in a secretive smile, eyes glittering with self-gratification.

"I talked with no reporter. Are you forgetting I've been in Spain?"

"No. But who on earth could have known any of the details of our relationship? You and Alan's father were all."

"You think so? Sorry to disappoint you, my schemer, but your former friend Alan was responsible for the call to the tabloid. You are probably responsible for devising the entire idea!"

146

"I most certainly am not!" she shot back boldly, hands on hips. Her eyes noticing his continued rubbing of his knuckles, she blurted out curiously, "Why are you doing that?"

"It feels good."

"Rubbing your knuckles?"

"Yes. An hour ago they were shoved into Alan's chin. I suspected him immediately of aiding and abetting you in your intrigue. He'll have plenty of time to repent while his broken jaw heals."

"You broke his jaw?"

"Yes. It should have been his neck but I admire his father too much for that. Now, about your punishment," he warned, his deep husky voice threatening as he started across the room.

"Mine!" Wary of his actions, she backed toward the door, intending to flee her apartment if he came any closer.

"Yours." His fists clenched at his side, he inched forward slowly, stalking her intensely.

Her auburn hair fired a vibrant halo around her exquisite face and shoulders as she faced him; her jade eyes glittered with fury when she raised her chin defiantly.

"I've done nothing!" she retorted arrogantly.

"Nothing, my sensuous surrogate? You dare say you've done nothing after I overheard each detail?"

Breasts rising and falling with the torment of his words, she made a dash for the door. But Derek had anticipated her behavior and lunged forward. Clasping De-Ann's narrow shoulders in his broad palms, he spun her around to face him. Her arm raised to strike his face but he grasped it in his palm and seized the nape of her neck with his other hand.

"Do you deny you told your mother the truth?"

Unshed tears glimmering in her wide eyes, she squirmed helplessly to break his hold.

"No," she answered truthfully before lowering her lashes.

Letting her wriggle until she was weary, he watched her determined struggles with admiration. Her inherent spirit was undaunted as she finally stood within his hold, expression proud.

"Finished?"

"With what?"

"Fighting me."

She nodded with reluctance, refusing to give him the satisfaction of hearing her voice his dominance.

Derek's punishing hold relaxed, softened into one of tenderness. His fingers caressed her neck and throat as his cobalt-blue eyes smoldered with unfulfilled desire.

Her heart beat rapidly and she felt that familiar clenching of her stomach at his touch. Ashamed at how quickly he caused her to lose control, she forced herself to face him rebelliously.

But Derek ignored the look and lowered his lips to the sensitive hollow of her neck, trailing wet kisses up to her lobe and flicking his tongue teasingly in her ear.

De-Ann lost all desire to fight him then, the fire in her jade-green eyes changing from fury to awakening passion. She molded her limbs to his hardened muscles.

He lifted her face upward, De-Ann's soft red lips parting unconsciously. Her fresh breath brushed his chin as she exhaled nervously. Any attempt to deny her response was futile in his clasp.

A low moan torn from his throat, Derek released De-Ann's palms. His hand slid over her spine until he felt each feminine curve pressed into his body. He shuddered with need—a deep aching need too long held in check.

The warmth of his long fingers smoothing her back

caused the familiar tingle of delight to extend through every nerve ending in her body. The hunger of his mouth as it took her lips in a relentless, searching kiss could be felt with each heaving breath of his powerful chest.

De-Ann's hands moved of their own accord to clasp his nape. Arching her body, she could feel his arousal beneath the fine cloth of his suit. She responded with the pent-up desire caused by Derek's long absence, but, afraid for him to see the love in her eyes, she drew away to burrow her flushed face against the cool silk of his shirt.

A featherlight caress touched the lustrous strands of auburn hair beneath his chin as he gripped her arms. Pushing her from him reluctantly, he exclaimed harshly, "You win, De-Ann, but the rules will be mine."

Her mind whirling with the electrifying sensuality of his kisses, she raised her slumberous eyes.

"I win . . . but with your rules. I don't understand," she murmured hesitantly.

"You will. You connived for the birth of my child! You devised a treacherous scheme to deceive and cheat me of my heir!" His voice harsh and forbidding, he continued cruelly, "We will marry as you wish. Wedding gowns, marriage licenses, and promises of eternal devotion, wasn't it?" His final taunt tore through her heart as he added coolly, "After the ceremony we play the game of wedded bliss *my* way."

Her heart breaking at the hostility of his words, she shook her head to stop him.

"No . . . no, Derek. Please, don't. I did it because I love you," she pleaded poignantly.

"You love me? Yet you dare deceive me behind my back. You sound no different from the women I've met in the past."

"No, Derek!" she cried, grasping his shoulders in her

small hands. "Don't think that, please. I could never act like they did."

"You already have. Anything a woman does to get a man to marry her does not surprise me now. I've had lessons in a woman's duplicity from professionals." He clenched his fists and groaned with anguish. "With you I was finally beginning to believe I was wrong."

After wrenching from her frantic hold on his biceps, he paced the living room floor as she slumped into an armchair. She trembled, waiting for more shocking statements. Remorse over her actions, the pain of knowing they had backfired, burned her heart like acid.

His continued silence tearing her heart, she finally blurted out poignantly, "What—what are you going to do to me, Derek?"

"I'm deciding. I have three weeks in Spain but I don't want you there now. Your presence would be too distracting."

He continued to pace, his big body dwarfing her living room, until he stopped before her. "After we're married, I'm going to drive you to my home in Hidden Coves. It's remote enough to make it difficult for you to leave."

"My God, am I to be kept prisoner until you find out I'm not like your father's wives or your mercenary girl friends?"

"Exactly! Until I can be with you, can assure myself of your fidelity, I want you cloistered in my seaside home. What happens between us after that, I will decide while I'm in Spain."

Jumping from the chair, she faced him. Her eyes, dark with temper, held his gaze. "I won't! You can't make me marry you, Derek Howell! I absolutely refuse to marry an arrogant, domineering man such as you!"

She ran to her bedroom in a sudden dash and tried to

lock the door, but Derek had followed her and, with his superior strength, shoved it open and entered.

Furious, Derek berated her. "Don't ever try to lock me out of a room again, De-Ann!"

"I will!"

"You won't or I'll throw you on that bed right now. After I'm finished slaking my long pent-up needs in your body, it won't matter how many plans you devise. I won't marry you—pregnant with my child or not!"

Turning her back to him, she fought for control. Her feminine instinct and strong independence told her to reject his arrogant terms, yet she knew deep within the innermost recesses of her heart that she could not. The only important thing was their marriage. What came later was insignificant in comparison to a life without him.

Deprived of Derek's proud aristocratic presence, De-Ann knew her fervent inner pleas would fail. Her hopes to forever erase the deep mistrust from his mind were dependent on the opportunity to give him her abundant love.

Refusing to bow to his cruel taunts, she turned to confront him. Her eyes were vulnerable as they locked with his questioning gaze.

"I'll marry you, Derek," she answered in a dignified voice.

"I thought you might when you thought it over," he added wryly.

Thinking he meant she wanted his wealth, she fired back, "I don't need you or any other man to support me, Derek. If you like, you can get Alan's father to draw up a prenuptial agreement. I'll be glad to sign over my rights to all of your money!"

"I realize that. Your unique talents are exceptional, as is your independence. Frankly, this deceitfulness regarding contracting with my attorney to be surrogate mother puzzles me. I had agreed there should be no contact. The woman's identity would remain confidential, as would mine. Your plan could have backfired, De-Ann. There was a distinct possibility that if you had disappeared I would never even have been aware you were the one who fled with my child."

"I was aware of that," she snapped, her temper still aroused.

"Yet you were still willing to go through with this scheme?" he questioned, his eyes trailing over her shapely figure as she faced him with fists clenched furiously.

"Yes."

"I must give you credit for ingenuity and originality. I've been sidestepping traps from scheming women for years now. All intent on getting their greedy hands on my wealth, yet you"—he pointed an accusatory finger at her —"you deceive to bear my child without my knowledge and agree to sign over all rights to every penny of my money!"

He paused, watching her intently, as she turned her back. Slender shoulders heaving with the force of her feelings, she was reminded of her mother's warning that the consequences of her own deceitfulness might not always be to her liking and she should share the blame if they weren't.

Tears were welled in her eyes when she turned to him. As if in slow motion she raised her face to meet his piercing gaze.

"I told you why."

"Because you love me?" he growled in disbelief.

"Yes."

"Prove it," he demanded huskily, his glittering eyes holding hers as tension mounted between them.

His eyes narrowed as her slender hands reached for the front of her blouse. Without hesitation she deliberately unbuttoned it. Lashes fluttering to hide her tear-filled eyes, she reached for the waistband of her skirt and slid it from her hips, letting it fall in a heap at her feet. As she stepped out of its soft folds she removed her sandals. Then, easing the sleeves from her arms, she pulled her blouse off and let it fall to the floor on her skirt.

Standing before him, clad in brief wisps of black lace, she inhaled at the look in his eyes. The darkened pupils had changed to the color of his raven hair as he drank in the sight of her ivory skin in bikini underpants and low-cut bra.

She swallowed hard in an attempt to control her heightened nerves and, turning her back, reached behind her to unfasten the clasp of her bra. Each motion was deliberate and unhurried. The casual ease belied the clenching of her abdomen, the tight feeling in her heart and mind.

Auburn hair shining vividly against the perfection of her slender back, she slipped the brief panties from her shapely hips. At the sound of his breath catching as she removed her last article of clothing, she turned.

With the grace of form inherent to her nature she slowly faced him. Chin held high, she stood proudly, hiding the twinge of shame she felt at her actions.

Creamy skin, unblemished and silky, was exposed in the soft light of the bedroom. Her breasts tautened beneath his gaze as she watched his eyes slide over her from the feathery strands of hair across her brow, downward over her mature curves, slender waist, untouched femininity, silken thighs, and small pink-tinted toenails. He stood in awe of her beauty.

"Come to me," he commanded in a husky voice.

Undaunted, De-Ann stepped forward, her hands reaching lovingly to clasp his nape.

"Undress me."

Without a word De-Ann let her hands fall to his jacket.

She eased it off his shoulders, then removed his tie before touching the buttons on his shirt. Deftly she undid each one until it was also a heap on the floor. Forcing herself to be calm, she avoided looking at the overpowering masculinity of his powerful chest. The scent of his body invaded her nostrils as she continued. With total nonchalance she placed her hands on his belt buckle. After undoing it, she reached for the button to his slacks when she was stopped by a low moan coming from Derek's throat.

"Enough. My God, you've proven your point now."

Taking her slender body into his arms, he pulled her to him. The feel of her swollen breasts crushed to the hard muscles of hair-roughened chest was unbearable as their naked torsos were joined in embrace for the first time.

"Oh, God, De-Ann, I need you so," he groaned, his face buried against the silken skin of her neck. The scent of her brought his body to the full peak of arousal as he rained fervent kisses frantically along her neck and shoulder.

The frustrations and anxieties of her days without him, of their problems yet to be faced, were wiped aside as she caressed his face between her palms. Holding it motionless, she raised her mouth until it was directly over his lips. Her tongue told him of her need as it flicked along his mouth until it could probe the hardness of his strong white teeth. Her fingers caressed each angle of his sharply molded face until his lips parted. Without restraint she let her innate sensuality guide her as she initiated a kiss so passionate, his body trembled beneath her hands.

Responding to her exploratory touches, Derek groaned with satisfaction at her sudden change of personality. The palpitations of her heart joined with his as the urgent need to dominate, to be the one to lead in lovemaking, overcame him. His arms raised to hold her, one trembling hand clasping her nape, the other running over the silky skin of her slender back. Fingers spread, he pulled her hips to him, caressing her firm buttocks as she arched upward to meet his seeking mouth.

Instinctively parting her lips, she submitted to each intimate touch without question, desperate to experience further exploratory caresses. Thoughts of morality were driven to the recesses of her mind as she gave her love to Derek without regret.

He lifted her in his strong muscular arms and placed her on the soft bed, then he lowered himself gently on top of her. His long length filled the single mattress as he cupped her body beneath him. One lean tanned hand caressed the length of her satiny legs; his mouth sought the erect tips of her breasts. Gently stroking the beauty of her hardened nipples with his warm tongue, he was aware the instant she surrendered her love into his keeping. His fingers quivered as they stroked upward, over her thigh, across the untouched erogenous apex of her body to her navel to end with the cupping of one exquisite breast.

Groaning, he raised his face to take her mouth in a fierce kiss, the hunger sending the blood coursing through their veins like wildfire. Torturous moments passed as he plundered the recesses of her mouth with his probing tongue before leaving to bury his face in the silky mass of hair tumbled about her shoulders.

Suddenly he raised himself from the bed, staring at her. The sight of tears trailing down her cheeks was his undoing. After buckling the belt of his slacks, he reached for his shirt. He casually buttoned the sleeves before starting over his chest.

"You win this round, De-Ann," he conceded, tucking the shirt into his slacks, his eyes never leaving her. "I never thought you would go through with it. When I trailed my hand over your—"

"No . . . please, don't say anything. I—I feel so ashamed as it is." She reached for the light bedspread and wrapped

155

it around her as the depth of her actions reached the consciousness of her mind.

"And you never flinched. I knew you were willing to give me anything I asked," he continued despite her pleas for silence. "The sight of your brimming eyes, the vulnerability of your innocence, were safeguards to your virginity as strong as the highest tower."

Watching while he shrugged into his jacket, she waited for his next move. She was afraid that her actions had driven him from her for good, so she sat up, ready to plead with him not to leave her.

"Don't go!" she cried out as he turned to leave the room.

Glancing at her pale face, the width of her lovely eyes, he took a deep breath before answering.

"I have to. One more minute in this room and I'll rape you."

"It—it wouldn't be rape," she admitted embarrassedly, her lashes lowered to shadow the thoughts in her mind.

"To me it would." Resting his head against the doorjamb for a moment, Derek murmured with the agony of a man fighting hard to control his innermost desires. "It would be rape in my mind, De-Ann. Despite the flaunting of your delectable body, the response of your awakening sexuality, to make love to you now would be like violating a sacrament. Your innocence protects you like a shield. I would be haunted for weeks if I took you knowing your aversion to premarital sex."

Turning to face her, he stood with fists tightly clenched along his lean thighs. "I find a sudden conscience extremely hard on my physical well-being and I don't like it!"

"What's going to happen between us now?" she pleaded desperately, afraid her worst dreams were about to come true.

"I'm flying back to Spain tonight. Complications have arisen on the project. I'll leave word with my personal secretary to get in touch with you."

"About what?" she questioned fearfully.

"Our wedding, of course! I want you to design our announcements, so get busy on it right away. We'll marry in two weeks."

"You're crazy." Her breasts heaving beneath the spread as she clutched it nervously, she asked, "Why will we need announcements anyway?"

His darkened eyes locked with hers and his deep voice filled the room. "You wanted the works and you'll get it. Enjoy your freedom, my lovely deceptive fiancée! The gold band you wanted so desperately will shackle you to me for life. I will tolerate neither infidelity nor divorce!"

Lifting his head, he regarded her with a grim smile tugging his lips. "Be warned, my love, my conscience will last only until the ceremony. After that, rest assured that these past weeks of frustration and enforced celibacy will be eased with vehemence!"

At his bold words De-Ann gasped and her small hands crossed over her breast. She watched his broad muscular back as he left the bedroom. Firm steps stopped momentarily before the sound of the door latching penetrated the room.

Clutching the spread to her naked body, De-Ann ran to the living room. She caught only a glimpse of Derek's white Ferrari as he pulled from the curb, the tires screeching and spinning on the hard pavement.

Tears trickled down her cheeks freely as she pondered her immediate future. Derek was willing to marry her but on his terms only. Her victory had also been her defeat.

When she returned to the bedroom to dress, her eyes were caught by the sight of a velvet jeweler's box. She opened it slowly and a cry of remorse escaped her lips as

157

she took the exquisite ring from its satin nest. Brilliant fire radiated from the huge oval diamond surrounded by a cluster of emeralds alternating with diamonds in the heavy gold setting.

An engagement ring befitting the world's most cherished bride yet tossed negligently on an end table as if a token afterthought.

CHAPTER NINE

"Miss Wagner?"

"Yes."

"I'm Harold Simpson, Mr. Howell's personal secretary. Derek requested I make arrangements to meet you at your earliest convenience. There are numerous details we need to discuss about your coming wedding. Would it be at all possible for you to have lunch with me today at one o'clock?"

De-Ann, impressed by Derek's secretary's soft-spoken voice, agreed readily. Placing the receiver on the cradle after a restaurant had been chosen, she leaned back in her office chair.

Derek continued to amaze her. His cynicism about women did not prevent him from being considerate of their comfort. Mr. Simpson had told her Derek insisted he send a taxi cab to pick her up so she wouldn't have to worry about parking in the heavy downtown weekday traffic.

Finishing with a logo design for a new stock-brokerage firm in Daly City, De-Ann placed it in a protective plastic

159

folder. Loud music blared from her radio, a deliberate attempt to help free her mind of the traumatic meeting with Derek the preceding Friday night—a necessity if she was going to complete her previous commitments before their marriage.

By working through the weekend, De-Ann had completed a design for their wedding announcements. The wastebasket beside the kitchen table where she worked in her apartment had been emptied twice, filled with unsatisfactory designs that had not met her stringent requirements.

Her moods had been mercurial, alternating between love and angry attempts at humor. Crossed swords over a frowning groom and tearful bride. An angry amazon character bride holding a shotgun to the head of a meek groom. Bride and groom with arms crossed, backs turned to each other in disgust. Each attempt at humor had failed miserably but had served the purpose of releasing some of the tensions from her troubled spirit.

After a restless weekend of deep introspection and soul searching De-Ann had decided to meet each obstacle as it arose. Determined to enjoy their wedding, knowing it would be her only one whatever the outcome, she gritted her teeth resolutely. The horrendous rift with Derek did not lessen her eager anticipation to be his wife.

Derek had proved the torment to her would be through mental frustration at his deep cynicism. Despite his arrogance and grimness toward her deceit he had treated her with tenderness. His hunger for physical release had been tightly checked despite the provocation and blatant advances she had made.

Aware she need never fear his touch, she knew she would be a receptive bride. To deny her new husband fulfillment could backfire in the worst possible way. With Derek's powerful masculinity and rugged handsomeness it would take little effort for him to find a willing consort anytime he desired.

Even thinking of Derek taking another woman made De-Ann frown with jealousy. Her heart pounded as she forced the image of their coming together as man and wife from her tormented mind. His lightest touch could set her body on fire with need and she could only imagine the beauty of the marriage consummation. To satisfy Derek's physical needs, she prayed, would lead to assuaging his mental well-being as well.

Applying a light touch of lipgloss, her smoothly brushed hair laying in shining waves about her shoulders, De-Ann looked up. The sound of screeching brakes in front of her shop made the driver's impatient tooting of his taxi's horn unnecessary.

She grabbed her purse and walked to the waiting taxi. A brief smile tugged the corners of her mouth when she noticed the appreciative gleam in the young driver's eyes, as he stared cockily over the top of the front seat.

Settling comfortably back, De-Ann smoothed the fine material of her teal-blue dress across her knees. Within minutes the reckless driver had pulled to the entrance of a luxury hotel with a rooftop garden restaurant. De-Ann rode the elevator to the top floor and gave her name to the courteous maître d'hôtel.

Escorted to a back booth, she ignored the visible admiration her appearance attracted. Auburn hair, cascading over her shoulders, glimmered with silken health, a perfect frame for her exquisite features. Small chin raised proudly, she walked with poise and grace. Her eyes locked with those of a gray-haired man several years Derek's senior, who stood waiting, hand outstretched in greeting.

Smiling, De-Ann took his hand, reassured the moment she looked into his kind hazel eyes. Dressed in a three-piece navy business suit, he appeared impeccable as he motioned for her to be seated.

Ordering each of them a drink, Derek's secretary relaxed in the plush booth. Momentarily silent, he contemplated the elegantly feminine girl his employer had decided to marry.

"I had intended to congratulate you, Miss Wagner, but after meeting you, I find Derek is the one to be congratulated. His taste in picking a bride cannot be faulted. You are exceedingly beautiful."

Harold's flattering words broke any social tensions of two strangers meeting for the first time. De-Ann laughed softly, her green eyes shimmering as she raised her shapely lips in an appreciative smile.

"Thank you, Mr. Simpson."

"Harold, please, De-Ann," he interjected quickly.

Her soft laughter was pleasing to hear. Eyes alight with humor, she told him truthfully, "I expected Derek would have a sexy blond female as his private secretary. You— you came as quite a surprise. A pleasant one, I might add."

"You don't know your future husband all that well then, De-Ann. He loathes females twittering around him during business hours. I act as go-between between him and all his adoring female staff." Lighting a cigarette, he inhaled slowly before continuing. "Derek's views are rather chauvinistic, I fear, in that regard. As you know, his home is also run by an all-male staff."

De-Ann was unaware of this, but she nodded in agreement, not wanting Harold to know she had only been to Derek's home for one brief, traumatic night.

Taking a sip of dry martini after stubbing his unfinished cigarette in the ashtray, Harold shuddered. "Another bad habit of mine. I should know better than to drink at lunch.

Alcohol never tastes good to me until after six o'clock at night."

"You should have ordered orange juice, Harold. This is delicious," De-Ann told him, taking a refreshing drink from her tall frosty glass adorned with a slice of lime and a bright red cherry.

After ordering lunch, they relaxed. The muted atmosphere was pleasant, making conversation easy yet providing privacy from other nearby diners.

"Are you aware of the plans for your wedding, De-Ann, or has Derek bulldozed right ahead without consulting you beforehand?" Harold inquired, both elbows resting comfortably on the edge of the table.

"Your implications are that my fiancé is a bully, Harold," she returned humorously, a thrill running through her body at calling Derek her fiancé.

"Never a bully. Just a man who insists on things being done his way. He has the keenest mind of anyone I have ever known. Derek's decisions are quick, concise, and invariably correct," Harold explained, looking at her with thorough contemplation.

"Very flattering."

"Not flattery at all, my dear, but the truth. I have held the deepest admiration for your fiancé since I first came to work for him over ten years ago. I could sit here the rest of the day and still not disclose all the kindnesses and charities your husband-to-be is involved with."

"I—I'm not aware of any of this. Derek never mentioned this side of his life to me at all," De-Ann explained. Her thick dark lashes covered the rush of love visible in her eyes on discovering this unknown side of Derek's personality.

Harold's laughter boomed out heartily as he watched De-Ann's expressive face. "I surprised you, didn't I? You above all others should know there's more to the man than

163

the fact that women find him irresistible. Derek's a complex person with the driving force and vigor of a dozen healthy men. He has not only burned the candle at both ends, my dear, he has seared the middle as well!"

"Now this part I had heard," she teased before jealousy made her change the subject abruptly.

Glancing sideways, they spotted their waiter wheeling a large serving cart with their lunch toward them. With a swooping flourish he placed a fluted shell-shaped bowl in front of De-Ann. A lavish shrimp Louis salad garnished with asparagus spears, olives, and marinated artichoke hearts over crisp lettuce pieces—it looked delicious. A plate of pink-tinged prime rib with fresh cooked vegetables was set before Harold. A cloth napkin kept hot slices of sourdough bread warm, waiting to be spread with iced curls of sweet butter.

"Looks tempting, doesn't it?" Harold asked, his fork already resting in the succulent beef as he prepared to cut a bite.

"Absolutely delectable! I've dined here several times and always found the food and service excellent." De-Ann speared a fat pink shrimp and, before placing it in her mouth, dipped it in the tangy seasoned Louis dressing. The firm sweetness of the cold cooked seafood was luscious, and she suddenly found herself starved.

Over the weekend, not wanting to spend time cooking, she had drunk endless cups of coffee for sustenance. She had worked long painstaking hours, immersed with each flawless detail until satisfied, seldom taking a dinner break.

After their lunch was finished, empty dishes removed, dessert declined, and drinks replenished, Harold leaned back, his eyes fastened on De-Ann with interest.

"Now to the details of your wedding and the purpose of our luncheon." Handing a typewritten sheet filled with pertinent details to De-Ann, Harold continued with further explanations for the forthcoming wedding.

Stunned, De-Ann listened, amazed by the speed of events that would join her to the man she loved. The wedding date was set for the Sunday after next. The church was chosen and contracted—complete with minister—the reception planned, hall rented, caterer and photographer hired, and guest list for Derek made up.

After reading the numerous preparations, De-Ann looked at the man across from her, her eyes wide and puzzled, her expression awe-filled.

"But—but how could all this possibly be arranged in such complete detail so soon? Derek didn't say anything to me until late Friday night. A brief three days ago!"

"As soon as I received a copy of the newspaper announcement of your wedding in the office mail, I contacted Derek in Spain."

"What—what did he say?" De-Ann asked plaintively. Leaning forward, she awaited Harold's answer breathlessly. Harold's phone call would have been Derek's first knowledge of the vindictively supplied gossip that had been anonymously planted by Alan.

"Oh, he apologized immediately for not telling me your plans earlier, then told me to get busy and make arrangements for your marriage at once." Harold smiled kindly. "Of course you know all this, plus the fact that he had already arranged to fly to you from Spain that night."

Dazed by Derek's calm acceptance of his secretary's shocking news, De-Ann clenched her empty glass nervously, her eyes lowered as she tried to fathom her fiancé's unusual actions.

"Did you design the announcements, De-Ann? Derek was emphatic that his fiancée's talents should adorn the invitations. The company printer is standing by to rush the order through. Extra help has been hired to print addresses on the envelopes when you've decided which style type you wish to use."

She reached into her large leather purse for the protective envelope and handed it to Harold. Her expression betrayed her anxiety as she asked, "Do you think this will be suitable?"

"Suitable! Derek has bragged constantly about your talents, but I just shrugged him off as a man very much in love. He was correct as usual." His eyes softened as he looked at De-Ann's rapt face awaiting his approval.

"The love you feel for Derek also shows through, my dear. You and he have obviously been blessed." His laughter was uninhibited as he leaned forward, adding smugly, "I warned him years ago his cynicism wouldn't last. He always scoffed at my teasing until he met you."

"What do you mean?" De-Ann inquired, her heart pounding at the thought that Derek had expressed his love for her to his secretary.

"He gave me a thousand-dollar bonus the day he met you. Told me I was right after all. That he had been struck down by a small bundle of fury with auburn hair and flashing green eyes."

Stunned by Harold's announcement, De-Ann blurted out with curiosity, "Do you remember the date?"

"Not exactly, but he did leave work early for the first time I can remember. Told me he had to return some clothes." Hand cupping his chin, he contemplated back in time. "Yes, now I remember. It was the night he made reservations for you at François's. I had never seen the man so distracted. All he could think of was getting to your office."

Insight to Derek's personality was being gained by each word from his secretary. De-Ann began to wonder if she should have been so harsh in her scorn of Derek's offer to provide for her as his mistress. It was obvious that it was as total a commitment Derek could have made to any woman until he felt secure that his love was returned with unquestionable fidelity.

"I remember also." She sat motionless, stunned that Derek had fallen in love with her so quickly. She took the cream-colored envelope that Harold held out to her and opened it, admiring the satiny gold inner lining and heavy bond paper card inside. With sensitive fingertips she stroked the finely textured quality paper. "This will make beautiful invitations, Harold. Very plush and uptown, to say the least." She laughed, her eyes bright with inner excitement.

"Can you get me your list of guests within three days?"

"I'll try. I'll contact my mother tonight, then make up my personal list. What's the limit?"

"Since there is so little time for people to prepare, Derek thought it best if we keep it down to three hundred plus however many you want to invite," he informed her calmly while removing a pen from his jacket pocket.

"Three hundred! That's not a wedding, it's a revival meeting."

"Your fiancé has hundreds of friends and business aquaintances around the world who would like to see his marriage." A smile tugged the corner of his mouth as he added wryly, "Most of them won't believe it unless they are there to witness the ceremony themselves!"

"What about my dress?" she sighed wearily, trying to comprehend the size of Derek's social and business world. "I suppose he'll want me to wear a traditional wedding gown?"

"Now, De-Ann," Harold teased with amusement, "can you actually imagine Derek wanting his bride to come to him in anything less than a long white gown?"

Smiling happily, she answered truthfully, "No. I've

167

heard reformed rakes make strict husbands. On top of that I have no illusions about Derek's chauvinism and ego."

"If you'll give me your mother's and father's full names and a few other pertinent details, I'll see to announcements in the leading newspapers around the world."

Then, handing De-Ann a card with the names and addresses of several exclusive stores, he added matter-of-factly, "Charge accounts have been opened for your trousseau. The checks from your new account will arrive at your home within the next two days. Ten thousand dollars has been deposited. Spend it as you wish." He added with a smile, "You've also been made sole heir in his will."

De-Ann's temper flared at Derek's assumption that she needed his money to pay for her clothes. Fists clenched, she leaned toward Harold, her eyes flashing sparks.

"Harold, I want you to contact Derek as soon as possible and remind him that I am *not* a pauper," she spluttered angrily. "I have never taken money from a man for clothes, nor do I intend to start now! As for his will—"

Admiring the spirit in the young girl across from him, Harold laughed humorously. "Derek said you had a quick temper, De-Ann. I'll let him know what you said, but if I had to lay odds on who wins most of the battles in your marriage, I'd bet on my boss."

"Well, don't bet too much, Harold. Derek is in for some trouble if he gets too bossy. I've been on my own for a long time, and not even that big brute will make me back down too often!"

"Honey, you won't ever have to argue with him. One smile, a gentle hand on his own, will soothe Derek's worst moods." Glancing at his watch, he added apologetically, "I have to leave. There are many things left to do today—including the call to Derek." He settled their bill and escorted De-Ann to a waiting taxi cab.

Having had the driver take her home instead of her

office, she became immediately involved with making a list of friends she wished to invite to the wedding. She phoned her mother and invited her to come stay for several days. De-Ann knew the numerous and hasty wedding preparations would be enjoyable if she could share them with her mother.

The rest of the week was spent in a flurry of shopping expeditions. For long exhausting days they traipsed in and out of San Francisco's shops, from the finest exclusive designer stores to small boutiques located on less popular side streets.

Discouraged by not finding the perfect dress, De-Ann was ready to return to her apartment when her energetic mother insisted she look at dresses in the final three stores on their list. Grumbling good-naturedly about her aching feet, she followed her mother to another small wedding shop.

The single gown displayed in the window brought a frown to De-Ann's face. She placed a hand on her mother's arm to stop her.

"Please, Mom. They always put their best dress in the window and that thing is positively awful! Let's go home and soak our feet."

"Hush now and quit your complaining. You have no patience," her mother scolded, brushing past De-Ann to enter the shop.

Mumbling under her breath about the days spent shopping when she had work to do at her office, she followed her mother's stout figure inside. Even more unhappy after seeing what was displayed before her, De-Ann sat on a small chair near the front window.

"I don't see a thing I like. You can browse through the place, but I absolutely refuse to move," she whispered as they waited for the saleslady to appear.

Handing De-Ann her purse, Mrs. Wagner glared at her

daughter's mutinous expression, then walked to the rear of the shop with short, determined strides. De-Ann watched her with amusement as she searched through rack after rack of wedding gowns while the saleslady watched nervously at her side. Declining the offer of assistance, she continued with her search to find her daughter's wedding gown.

De-Ann's lashes lowered to conceal the brief look of misery she felt thinking of Derek. Despite each moment being filled with things to accomplish, she ached for the sight of his broad frame, yearned to hear his voice and see the look in his eyes as they rested on her—whether it be in anger or love.

"Wake up, De-Ann. I found your dress."

Her mother's voice roused her from her reverie. She opened her eyes to see yards of ivory satin and lace carefully cradled in the woman's arms. De-Ann reached for the gown, touching its soft folds lovingly before smiling at her mother.

"It's perfect, Mom. Absolutely my dream dress come true," she sighed, happiness shining in her eyes.

Once in the dressing room at the rear of the shop De-Ann stripped to her cinnamon-hued lace bra and briefs, chuckling at her mother's shocked face when she observed the sensual underclothes.

"We've come a long way since cotton shirtwaists, Mom. Help me with my dress," she asked, arms raised over her head as her mother carefully slipped the gown into place. A sheer illusion neckline with a dainty stand-up collar accented the fitted bodice and sheer sleeves trimmed with imported Alençon lace. Hundreds of seed pearls were hand sewn across her breasts, around the tiny waist, pointed cuffs, and soft folds of the flowing skirt hem, matching those on her veil.

Turning around, De-Ann smiled dreamily. "Thank you

for finding it for me, Mom. It's everything I ever wished for."

"I knew I'd find it here," her mother said smugly, dabbing her eyes. "Now, have them deliver it, then you can take me to lunch. You've run me ragged all week and I'm tired."

Laughing at her mother's sudden change of attitude, De-Ann changed into her street clothes. When it came time to write the check, she barely hesitated at the shocking price, pleased that she hadn't needed Derek's money.

As soon as they returned to the apartment after a satisfying lunch, De-Ann slipped off her high-heeled sandals with a sigh of relief. Packages heaped carelessly on the couch, she padded into the kitchen to make coffee while her mother freshened up.

Clad in a favorite robe, feet tucked under her, De-Ann relaxed with a steaming cup of coffee. Smiling, she exclaimed happily, "We did it, Mom. My trousseau's complete. Next week I can close out my office."

"What are you going to do with all your supplies, De-Ann?" her mom queried, comfortable in a soft armchair with her feet propped up.

"I've been debating. I don't have room in my apartment, yet I hate to part with anything. I worked so hard decorating the office, making the rug and wall hangings. . . . Guess I'll store my things in a warehouse until I find out where my opinionated fiancé wants me to set up shop."

"I can hardly wait to meet my new son, honey. You've talked about him constantly this past week. I must say he sounds like he's perfectly capable of controlling your impetuosity."

Noticing her mother's coffee cup was empty, De-Ann rose, taking it with her own to the kitchen for refilling. As she reached for cream and sugar to fix her mother's coffee, the phone rang. She didn't expect a call, so she told her mother to answer it. Returning to the living room, deftly balancing both brimming cups in their saucers, she heard her mother speaking.

"Why, Son, it's absolutely marvelous to meet you even if it's over the phone." Placing her hand over the mouth-piece, her eyes twinkling, she whispered to De-Ann, "It's Derek, honey. Oh, I love him already just hearing his deep voice." Returning to Derek, her mother ignored De-Ann completely as she talked with her future son-in-law.

De-Ann's heart pounded with the anticipation of talking to Derek. She waited impatiently while her mother's animated voice continued nonstop for a full twenty minutes.

"Here, De-Ann. Derek wants to talk with you now," she added calmly, handing her daughter the receiver.

Her voice barely above a whisper, De-Ann cradled the phone in her hand as she listened to Derek's voice after a brief hello.

"De-Ann, I'm phoning you for three reasons. One: Lay off Harold. He's been singing your praises to where I'm sick of it, yet you only met him one time. He may be my secretary but he's a man first and must be wondering what it would be like to take you to bed too!"

Shocked by his words, she hissed angrily, pleased that her mother was in the bathroom and couldn't hear. "Derek Howell, you're a beast! And what do you mean by 'too'?"

" 'Too' meaning myself, my secretary, and any other red-blooded male who sees you, including that namby-pamby Alan!" Continuing with his reasons, he added furiously, "Two: Why the hell did you send your checks back to Harold? That is your money and you'll damn well spend it. We'll do a lot of entertaining and traveling and

172

I insist your wardrobe be the envy of any woman you meet!"

"Tough! I'll darn well wear what I want, wherever I want, and when I want. No man will ever tell me how to dress nor buy my clothes, for that matter, if I don't want it!" It was hard to keep her voice to a scornful whisper; she shook with rage.

Interrupting, he continued, "Three: The design for our wedding announcements is very beautiful. A bride and groom silhouetted before an arched stained-glass window surrounded by streaking rays of sunshine is another example of your unique talent."

His honest and enthusiastic praise abated the momentary anger caused by his arrogant attitude, and she smiled. "It's a good thing I threw away the first ones I drew!"

"I can imagine. With your scheming mind and fiery temper—"

Breaking off his comment, she blurted out, "Have you decided what you're going to do about us? After the wedding, I mean."

"I'm taking you north as planned. In eight days' time your virginity will be nothing but a memory by the time the clock strikes midnight."

"Maybe and maybe not, Mr. Derek Howell. I'll marry you as planned but I'll darn well make up my own mind when or if I want to go to bed with you!" Determined to stand up to him, she bravely sassed him despite his blatant warning.

"You're very brave with me in Spain. Your threats are worthless in my presence, so be prepared to take the consequences for your wayward tongue!" He changed the subject abruptly, his voice softening. "Tell your mother I'm anxious to meet her. No one—not even my own father —ever called me Son."

His admonition to behave herself until their wedding

ringing in her ears, De-Ann hung up the phone. Heart filled with pain, she thought of the lonely childhood Derek had experienced. His surging into manhood while still a child had contributed to his distrust of women. Denied the love of a mother, he would receive ample from his future mother-in-law. Derek would be one more person enfolded in the loving arms of her mother, whose heart overflowed with love for all God's creatures. De-Ann smiled as her mother entered the room.

"I already love that boy, De-Ann, and I'm ashamed that you ever thought you could deceive him. You've always had a mind of your own and been too independent for your own good, but I'll guarantee you, my son will keep you in line," her mother warned her while methodically straightening De-Ann's packages.

"Your son? He's a son-in-law-to-be, Mom," she retorted impudently, miffed that her mother was siding with Derek already.

"He's my son. I don't believe in this in-law stuff. I intend he call me Mother. I also gathered that his promise to the paper to have an heir within the first year will be true."

"Well, now, I'll have some say about that!" De-Ann blurted out.

"I very much doubt that too," her mother added with a smile over her shoulder as she carried lacy underwear in jewel-tone colors into De-Ann's bedroom. "If he decides you'll have his child, I would imagine he'll have no trouble persuading you he's right."

Grabbing a handful of packages, De-Ann followed her mother, a faint flush staining her cheeks as she placed a new three-piece suit on a hanger. "Well, maybe you're right this time, Mom. He can be—er—pretty convincing physically when he sets his mind to it."

"Turns you on, does he?" her mother spoke matter-of-factly, surprising De-Ann with her turn of phrase.

"Mother dear, that man flat turns me inside out. If you knew how close I came to going to bed with him before marriage, you'd be ashamed of me." Sitting cross-legged in the middle of her narrow bed, she sighed wistfully. "He's also the reason I waited all these years to give myself to a man. Deep in my heart I knew I wouldn't be able to live with my own conscience comfortably if I couldn't go to my husband a virgin."

"I'm glad you feel that way, honey. Not so much because your father and I taught you to believe that way but because your first love is a precious gift to give. Much too precious to lose in the momentary heat of a casual affair."

"I agree. Now tell me what my arrogant fiancé told you he had planned for my future."

De-Ann shook her head, perplexed, as her mother explained each detail that Derek had meticulously worked out for his fiancée's final week prior to the wedding. With careful thought Derek had planned that each problem facing her would be solved.

His consideration for her had reached out across the sea to comfort her despite his resolution to punish her for the deceitful attempt to conceive his heir.

CHAPTER TEN

Standing for a moment to reflect on the past week's activities, De-Ann found it hard to believe that she was married. Wearing a white scalloped-edge bra and lacy designer underwear by Givenchy, she sighed. "It's unreal, Mother. Look at this bedroom, the entire house, my wedding."

Walking to the built-in closet along one wall of the bedroom, which was larger than her entire apartment had been, she hesitated, looking over her shoulder.

"You really do like him, Mom, don't you?"

Mrs. Wagner, clad in a bright rose two-piece dress with a white orchid corsage pinned over her bosom by Derek, smiled with pleasure. "Yes, my only daughter, I like your husband. I also love him as my new son." Placing De-Ann's wedding gown and finery in a protective bag, she sniffed, unashamed that tears filled her eyes. "You've a big job ahead, De-Ann. Derek's a man who will take careful handling. He's not used to a woman's love or gentle touch. It will be your responsibility to replace the distrust in his mind with love."

"I know, Mom. Derek had a miserable childhood and

it's left deep scars. It makes me cry thinking of all the love you and Dad gave me, yet Derek received nothing! Nothing at all from either his unfaithful mother or bitter father."

After tightening the belt at her waist, she adjusted the white silk of her blouse and tied a neat bow at her throat. Slipping on the rust-colored vest of her new three-piece suit, she stood before the mirror. The rust and jade plaid skirt in a wraparound style looked smart yet would be comfortable during their long drive north to Derek's seaside home.

De-Ann's mother helped her slip the jade-green jacket over her slender shoulders. "You look beautiful, honey. Smell good too! I've never seen so many cosmetics in a bathroom in my life. The bedroom is certainly masculine-looking, though."

"Derek says I can redecorate the entire house when I—er—we return from our . . . honeymoon," she explained, adding a final spray of perfume to her wrists and throat. Aware of Derek's cynicism to marriage, De-Ann's mother had no idea he was angered with her daughter and intended to cloister her in his coastal home as punishment. She assumed the two of them were planning a long honeymoon together in complete accord.

Unbidden tears making her eyes luminous, De-Ann hugged her mother, unaware that Derek had entered the room, impatient to leave. The sudden frisson of emotion that always warned her of his presence caused her to glance upward, her widened eyes wary.

Her lashes fluttered shut in a vain attempt to conceal the sudden rush of love for her new husband. Dressed casually in brown slacks and a cream-colored body shirt, he walked forward. With obvious affection he bent to hug the ample figure of his mother-in-law before placing a kiss on each powdered cheek.

177

His eyes raised to lock with De-Ann's, the smoldering fire in their depths warning her of his thoughts. His months of self-denial had reached the end. His expression let her know he would no longer suppress his hunger for release in her arms.

"Are—are you ready to leave now, darling?" De-Ann asked hesitantly, cheeks tinted a soft rose. Despite knowing Derek for many weeks, she had never called him by an endearment before. The words of love she often ached to use were all whispered in the uninhibited recesses of her mind. Her thoughts had been allowed full rein, letting her vocabulary of love grow without restraint.

"Oh, yes, my precious wife. I'm ready . . . to leave!" he replied huskily, one eyebrow raised high.

Understanding his double-edged meaning, De-Ann glanced away nervously from the searing look as his eyes surveyed her entire figure, their gleam showing approval.

One last kiss from her mother and she turned to Derek. Her chin held high in warning that she would not kowtow to harsh treatment without an attempt at opposition, she faced him proudly.

With a broad palm he cupped her shoulder, guiding her to the door of his room, his other arm around her mother's waist. They walked three abreast down the broad hall to the foyer. There they said their tearful good-byes.

Moments later De-Ann was seated in the front of the white Ferrari. Clenching her hands, she held them in her lap, attempting to stop their trembling. A sudden nervousness made her throat dry, caused her to swallow to ease the discomfort. She glanced at Derek as he shifted forward to ease from the broad driveway of her new home.

"Derek?"

"What, no 'Derek darling' now that we're alone? Don't tell me there's already a rift in the marriage and we've only

178

been married"—he checked his watch and glanced briefly at his bride's bowed head—"four hours."

Turning her gaze to him again, she reached with a soft touch to his muscular forearm. "Could we call a truce for today? I—I don't think I could stand it if our first day was spent in anger. I've dreamed of this moment since I was a young girl and I don't want you to spoil it for me by venting your anger."

"You're forgetting something, dear wife. Your scheming, despicable plan to force this marriage or keep my child from me if I didn't fall in with your plans is the reason for my anger!"

De-Ann watched with disinterest as they wound through the traffic toward the Golden Gate Bridge. "I realize that, Derek. I'm willing to accept the blame for my attempts to dupe you." Facing him, she added softly, "You must accept your share in our discord also. It's your misogynistic beliefs that were our final problem."

"Mysogynistic! How could that be? I absolutely love women!" he retorted, manuevering through the increased traffic toward the turnoff to California's coastal Highway One.

"Love to you means sex. To me it means a lifetime commitment to living a monogamous existence until . . . death do us part!" Voice breaking, she was unable to hold back the tears. They trickled down her cheeks unchecked.

"My God, don't cry! I'll agree to anything you wish for the day, but I warn you I'm still bitter at the thought that you—the only woman I've ever loved—contrived behind my back to force my hand." His hands, clenching the steering wheel, tightened until his knuckles were white, as he taunted her with anger. "Instead of giving you my love freely, I'm filled with bitterness at your deceit!"

Sobs tearing her apart, she trembled, feeling as if the

world had tumbled about her feet. Biting back words that might cause further discord, she forced herself to remain quiet and relax. She knew the journey to his home would seem like a lifetime. Taking a tissue from her purse, she sniffled quietly.

Long uncomfortable moments passed as Derek paid close attention to his driving on the tortuous mountain road. Suddenly he pulled to a stop in a layby.

The sight of her dejected figure had torn into his heart. With tender hands he reached out to pull her to him, his broad palms cradling her against his heaving chest.

"You win. From this moment our wedding day will be filled with the happiness we felt until I asked you to be my mistress." Unable to control the impulse, he kissed the satiny strands of silk beneath his chin, his body shuddering at the scent of her hair and skin.

Cherishing the minutes in close contact, De-Ann raised her eyes, love shining in their depths as she touched her husband's cheek. With tender fingers she caressed the hardness of his jaw before clasping his neck.

"We haven't been together in joy since the wondrous night at the concert. Until that night each moment together had been bliss." She kissed his chin, pulling on his nape to reach his mouth.

Jerking from her touch, he warned her, "I—I want you so desperately, De-Ann, that I'm unable to control a casual caress. It's been weeks since I've held you. Weeks with the image of your delectable nakedness imprinted on my brain. Long torturous weeks of physical frustration aching for release. An uncomfortable feeling that will soon be eased!"

"It hasn't been easy for me either, Derek. You awakened me to the needs of my body too! Ones only you can satisfy," she explained truthfully, unashamed to admit she wanted him with a passion nearing his.

"How foolish you are, De-Ann. You're not so naive that you aren't aware physical release can be experienced with a variety of partners," Derek stated as he pulled out onto the highway. Unable to take his eyes from the road as they drove hundreds of feet above the surging Pacific Ocean, he laughed hoarsely. "If that wasn't so, there would be no need for the world's oldest profession!"

Angered by his bluntness and his audacity at thinking she could think of permitting another man to touch her, she blurted out, "If that's so, then why are you in such bad physical shape? Apparently you never had the problem of unrequited desire before we met!"

"True. Sexual gratification was the least of my problems before I saw you for the first time." His voice lowering to a husky baritone, he explained honestly, "Since meeting you, I've never considered taking another woman. You've entranced me so, that I doubt if I could even function satisfactorily. I want only you—and I shall have you tonight!"

De-Ann was unable to hide the elation that she felt knowing she had penetrated his heart to that extent. His blunt words gave her the hope she needed, filled her with the reassurance necessary to get through the rest of their wedding day.

She changed the subject, her basic cheerfulness helping to ease the mounting tension between them.

"I haven't had time to thank you for everything you did for me to make the last week easier." Eyes lingering on his handsome profile, she smiled. "I was really in a dilemma until Harold called, surprising me with the announcement that you arranged for me to move my supplies to your home."

"Do you like the room?"

Unconsciously fingering the unaccustomed weight of her wedding ring, she enthused, "It's marvelous. High above the city with a view of the bay—what more could I ask? Mom helped me arrange my plants and wall coverings. Your movers placed my office desk and worktables where I wanted them. I even brought the display counter with me. You'll have to see how it looks when we—when *you* go back."

"Will you want to work when you return from Hidden Coves?" he questioned, proud of her independence and talents.

"Yes, of course." Enjoying the rolling pastures as they drove inland for several miles, she answered without taking her eyes from the view. "I don't want to open a shop, though. I've struggled for five years dealing with the public. If you don't mind, I'd like to do free-lance calligraphy. I'm going to illustrate and hand-letter a children's fairy tale up north. I find more satisfaction with that than doing menus and wedding invitations."

"Will you work for me? I'll pay you more than you charge now," he said matter-of-factly.

"I don't want to be an employee of yours," she replied grimly.

"Why?"

"It doesn't fit with my ideas of marriage. I grew up in a home where everything was done as a partnership. Mom wouldn't have thought of charging Dad for helping him in his office nor paying me for mowing the lawn. Tasks were accomplished with pride and a desire to help the family."

Brows drawn together, Derek contemplated De-Ann's words. Her willingness to give of herself to him was a constant surprise, unlike any relationship he had known in the past.

"Will you be my partner?" he queried, shocking himself with his sincerity. He had never considered a partnership; he had found satisfaction in solitude. Nor had he expected to be so infatuated with a woman that he would respect her ideas. Derek's mind was unsettled. He wanted to open his soul, but a lifetime of wariness made him hold back despite his love for his new wife.

Watching his expression, seeing he was sincere, De-Ann shook her head. "No. Being your wife is the only partnership I need."

"Meaning?"

"Meaning my love for you will be a full-time job," she shot back without thinking.

"Love?"

"Yes, love. I've never tried to hide the fact that I've given you my heart. You're just not ready to accept it."

"You amaze me," he told her, considering her words carefully. "Your pledges of devotion could convince a younger, less determined man."

"Less cynical, you mean," she mocked, eyes flashing.

"Truce, remember?" he reminded her, deep in retrospection.

"I should! It was my idea," she sassed impertinently before giving him a wide smile. His laughter filled her with tenderness, reminding her of the rapport they had shared before their disagreements.

Herds of large black-and-white holstein dairy cattle grazed the rolling green hills on irrigated pastures. Adjoining fields confined herds of smaller brown jersey cows, some already lining up to be stripped of their rich milk.

Studying the changing scenery as Derek drove along the edge of Tomales Bay, De-Ann told him impetuously, "I was going to buy a home in Bodega Bay after our argument. I spent a weekend looking at property but couldn't find anything affordable."

"It's a good thing because you would have just had to sell it. If you live along this coast, it will be with me in my development."

183

Slowing the powerful motor of his Ferrari, Derek drove carefully through the tiny town of Bodega Bay. An enchanting town dotted with small private boats and fishing vessels across its blue bay, it was picturesque enough to become world famous as the setting for *The Birds,* Alfred Hitchcock's suspense-filled movie. Its misty bird-filled marshes were appropriate to the thrilling tale.

"Did you get to see Cristo's 'Running Fence' before the wind destroyed it?" Derek motioned with his arm to show her a herd of sheep grazing after mentioning the renowned artist.

"Yes. I loved it, although it was considered controversial and was tied up in bureaucratic red tape for months. A group of us drove up to take photographs and picnic. The breeze was whipping the white nylon, causing it to ripple as it undulated across the hills for miles and miles. Great fun!"

"Male or female group?"

"Both."

"Too bad we don't have a camera and picnic lunch," Derek stated ruefully. "Do you want to stop somewhere for lunch or did you have enough at the buffet?"

"I didn't eat anything." Smiling smugly, she informed him, "You know, we do have a picnic lunch. Mom and I were so fidgety last night, we both vented our nervousness in the kitchen. Mom baked bread and I baked my speciality."

"Which is?"

"Upside down apple pie, with plump walnuts and brown-sugar glaze."

"I've never heard of upside down pie before. Sounds good, though."

Noticing a viewing area ahead, De-Ann put her hand on Derek's knee and felt the muscles tighten instantly. Flushing, she removed it before asking, "Let's stop, Derek. For a few minutes anyway."

Agreeable, Derek drove across the highway to park. Easing his broad shoulders against the seat, he turned to De-Ann. "Want to get out or relax inside the car?"

"Get out, of course!" She stepped to the edge of the rock guard rail and looked down the cliff to the deep blue Pacific Ocean crashing in a whirl of foamy lace against the jagged coastline cliffs.

Inhaling the tangy salt-laden air whipping around her face, she was uncaring of her skirt as it blew up to expose a tantalizing glimpse of satin-smooth thigh. Blazing auburn, her lustrous hair was soon a mass of tumbled waves.

Her eyes shimmering with pleasure, De-Ann smiled at Derek. "Beautiful is too common a word to describe anything as glorious as this view, isn't it?"

Derek watched her closely for a moment before speaking in an intimate voice. "Yes, my wife. . . . Beautiful is far too common a word."

Making a face at him to break the sudden seriousness of his mood, she laughed. "Not me, crazy! The ocean and the shoreline."

"You're the only thing I want to look at today." His voice suddenly gruff, he commanded. "Let's go. We're less than an hour from my home. We'll eat your picnic lunch there."

De-Ann, undaunted by his mercurial moods, complied without protest. Once seated in the car she took her make-up kit from the roomy shoulder purse at her feet and added a touch of lipstick before smoothing her hair about her shoulders.

"I didn't realize you traveled with such regal company, Derek. My head's still whirling trying to remember all the political dignitaries and members of high society who attended our wedding. I can't believe Nick and Carlyn flew in from Italy."

"They're all my friends and, I might add, eager to become better aquainted with you." His brief glance took in the beauty of her profile as she watched the changing view through the front windshield. "It will take us a year to entertain all the people who honored us with their presence . . . and presents."

"Oh, that's wonderful! I'd love to give parties in your home."

"Our home!"

"In *our* magnificent home," she corrected, "they'll be sheer delight. I never had room for more than two or three couples at a time." Already planning ahead, she suddenly thought of Derek's longtime servants.

"Do you think Charlie or Smitty will mind me living there?" she asked shyly, aware of what a drastic change her appearance would be.

"Charlie and Smitty! Good Lord, if you've got to that stage of familiarity this soon, they'll obviously work eagerly to satisfy each feminine whim." Shaking his head, Derek sighed with amazement. "Those two have the reputation of being the stuffiest household employees in San Francisco. No one is allowed to address them so informally."

"I find that hard to believe. They're just a couple of old tender-hearted softies," she teased mischievously, her voice pert. "They're the cutest brothers I've ever met. One dark, one fair. Hmm . . ."

Unable to curb a sudden surge of jealousy, Derek scowled with anger. "It's a damn good thing I'm taking you north then. If you admire them so much, you may never leave my coastal home!"

"Oh, Derek don't be angry. I was only teasing you." Reaching to console him, she implored, her small hand gripping his arm, "I love you, Derek. Only you for the rest of my life. I couldn't bear it if I had to watch what I say for fear you'd react jealously."

Derek's jaw tightened with determination as he forced the cynicism that tormented him from his mind. Easing his foot from the gas pedal, he brought the Ferrari back to a safe speed for the highway.

"I'm not jealous," he lied, attempting to reassure her. "Love can mean many things to many people. People can love a movie, an animal, a joke, or a ball game. None of which means the same as the love of a man for his wife."

De-Ann's eyes filled with awe and she looked at Derek. "I know, darling, but it's the love I feel for you that makes the other loves unimportant."

"We shall see."

De-Ann watched as Derek's fingers clenched the steering wheel and his lips tightened into a grim line.

"I heard my stepmother declare eternal love to my father one hour before she came to my room seeking 'love' from me. I vowed then I would never tell a woman I loved her."

"You've told me that many times," she reminded him softly.

"I know. I've said and done many things with you that I'd vowed I never would," he shot back impatiently. "Including marriage!"

Her volatile temperament flared despite her vow to contain it. "That does it! Before this farce of a marriage goes any further, you can take me to my apartment. Have Alan's father draw up annulment papers and we'll part permanently."

"On what grounds?" Derek asked calmly.

Eyes flashing angrily at him, she raised her chin. "That the marriage was never consummated!"

"It wouldn't be true," he continued in a surprisingly soft voice, each word enunciated clearly.

"It most certainly would! Frankly I'm sick and tired of hearing how you've been tricked into marriage. No one held a shotgun to your head that I could see!"

Derek smiled at the fury on her small face as she sat mutinously in the corner, refusing to meet his eyes. His laughter boomed through the car.

"You little shrew! Do you think I would give up the opportunity to change all that fury into passion?" Checking his watch, he reminded her arrogantly, "In five or six hours there won't be a judge in the world who would grant you an annulment!"

Her efforts to ignore him futile, she stared straight ahead, her back stiff against the cushioned seat, breasts heaving with agitation at the power he had over her emotions.

"I—I hope it's terrible!" she stormed.

"What? Loving you?" he teased, enjoying their fray.

"No. The darned apple pie!"

Shaking his head in disbelief, he drove competently toward their destination. "Who in the hell cares about apple pie now?"

"You will when your big brawny frame needs sustenance!"

"The only thing my big brawny frame needs is you!" he shot back, his features perfectly controlled.

"Well, then quit being so darn arrogant, Derek Howell. I managed perfectly well before I met you and I can do so again!"

"Maybe. Maybe not. You won't get the chance to find out. You're mine. Every soft, sweet particle."

Inwardly De-Ann was pleased that he desired her but she was also angered that he could infuriate her so quickly. *It always seems to be like this with him,* she thought. *One*

188

minute I'm filled with love for him and the next my blood boils with rage. Why does he confuse me so?

Silently she watched the miles speed by. A brief spasm made her stomach clench, knowing they would soon reach his home. Mixed feelings of apprehension and expectation ran through her mind as she thought of what lay ahead. Twisting her wedding ring around her finger, she was unaware Derek observed her sudden nervousness.

"Don't worry about it before it happens."

"Wh-what?"

"The consummation of our marriage. You're mature, healthy, and inherently passionate. Your past responses to me will make your first experience easy unless you tighten up with nerves or attempt to assert your independence by fighting me."

"I—I told you I wouldn't fight you, Derek, but I expect you to treat me with respect."

"Have I ever harmed you, De-Ann?"

"Not physically. Mentally you've caused me weeks of anguish."

"It all evens out fairly, I'd say. I've had weeks of physical anguish. Who's to say which is worse?" Pointing ahead, he told her to observe closely, as they were nearing his development.

She observed the first of miles of the split-rail fencing that surrounded the acreage of Derek's Hidden Coves land development. Weathered by the seasons, the fence looked as natural as the ungrazed wild grasses growing profusely among the scattered trees.

Precipitous cliffs wound upward to the east of the highway, making a spectacular backdrop for the vast amount of flat or gently sloping meadowland.

Gratified by the expression of awe, the wonder showing in her face as she leaned forward, Derek swung through the broad gates to enter Hidden Coves. Inspiring envy to many, to Derek it was home. A feeling of peace was already around his broad shoulders. Waving at one of his caretakers raking the broad expanse of lawn surrounding the cluster of stores and offices that made up the heart of his development, he sighed with satisfaction.

They traveled past a scattering of weathered homes, all unique in architecture but designed to harmonize with their environment. Derek drove on, leaving the settlement far behind. He wound through a forest of windswept trees toward a sturdy home sitting solid and content on a private stretch of land jutting out to the sea.

Stopping in the sheltered area in front of a wide garage, Derek turned to De-Ann. "We're home," he declared with pride.

De-Ann's eyes widened at the aesthetic rarity of his home with its matchless architecture. Derek had managed to build a coastal paradise without losing any of the beauty of the natural environment. She remained speechless as he took her by the arm to the wide front door. His home appeared to be a haven of tranquillity from the bustle and noise of the city. Traffic noises had been replaced by the sound of the ocean below and angry twittering of a scrub jay.

Unexpectedly she was swung high into Derek's arms. Clinging to his nape, she lay her head against his neck. A surge of love flowed through her body knowing that she was bound for life to the complex man holding her so gently as he entered his seaside home.

Eyes tender with adoration, she stared at the strength of his features.

Turning quickly he caught her look, his eyes smoldering with the force of his desire. With deliberate slowness he bent his head until his breath was a warm draft on her face. His lips hovered over hers for long torturous seconds, until he could no longer hold himself back.

"My wife . . . oh, God, how I want you!"

Powerless to resist him, she stroked his nape, her lips raised to receive the pleasure of his kiss—their first kiss since the impersonal salute he had given her after their marriage.

With hunger he took her mouth, his lips clinging as they moved hungrily over the sweetness beneath them. Her slender weight unnoticed, he held her to his chest, standing with legs braced barely inside the opened front door.

Responding with feelings long denied, De-Ann parted her lips to meet the increasing demand of his passion. Soft whimpers of bliss escaped her throat as their needs elevated. Humbled by the power she had to arouse her husband, she paid little attention as he set her on her feet, his broad palms drawing her body to the full length of his own. Arched to meet his needs, she was suddenly released.

Hands clenched at his sides, knuckles taut, wide chest heaving, Derek shuddered. "Not yet, my wife. I've waited for this moment for months. It shouldn't hurt me to bide my time until I've unpacked the car, checked to see the house is okay, and fed you dinner."

His footsteps sounded loud in the silence of the empty entranceway as she willed her heart to slow down. She tried to control the desperation she felt away from his arms. Walking forward, she entered the wide front room that ran the entire width of the house. Sparsely furnished, it looked masculine yet comfortable with its broad oversize couch and deep leather armchairs pulled before a gigantic fireplace waiting for the stroke of a match to its dried logs. Gleaming oak floors were visible around the edges of the soft pile rug in the center of the long room.

Hearing Derek return, she twisted around in time to see him set down their suitcases in the tiled foyer. "There's no television!"

"I know. No television, no phones, no outside news

unless you go to the main office. The people who build here want to get away from the pressures of the city. Instead of television you find libraries with books that have been read. Without phones you find your blood pressure lowering and ulcers healing. This is a second-home colony that satisfies needs that our cities can't."

"No television or phone won't bother me. I'll enjoy being able to work on my illustrations without any interruptions."

"Not tonight you won't!" he warned her emphatically. "Come, I want to show you the rest of the house, then we'll unpack. We'll have time for a walk to the end of the bluff before it's dark. I have a hundred-and-eighty-degree white-water view."

Two hours later, invigorated by the walk around the edge of Derek's bluff seventy feet above the surging ocean, they relaxed in Derek's cozy kitchen, having enjoyed the tasty picnic made by De-Ann and her mother. Watching Derek eat his second piece of apple pie, De-Ann smiled.

"Do you like it?"

"Hmmm . . ." Chewing the last bite with relish, he grinned. "Can you bake bread as delicious as your mother's?"

"Naturally. My mother insisted I learn to cook, clean, balance a checkbook, and keep quiet when the man of the house had problems to solve," she told him smugly.

"Successful on three counts isn't too bad. I can't imagine you being quiet for long," he taunted, relaxedly sipping a freshly brewed cup of coffee.

De-Ann sensed that Derek was deliberately biding his time in an effort to help her relax. He had made no attempt to touch her during their tour of his house, despite the intimacy of the loft bedroom that directly overlooked the rugged coastline. They had walked companionably across the meadow grass surrounding his home, the conversation informative but impersonal.

Appreciative of his consideration to avoid any awkwardness, she watched covertly through her thick lashes. He leaned back in the comfort of a kitchen chair, his wide shoulders outlined beneath the thin material clinging to the rippling muscles.

She was suddenly filled with an overwhelming desire to know everything about her husband. With intense interest she questioned him about his most prized project, the Hidden Coves development.

"Derek, why did you build on this land?" Holding the base of her coffee cup in both hands, she watched the dark liquid dreamily as he expounded his reasons.

"I was fortunate enough to have the opportunity to purchase this amount of land in its natural state. My restrictions will see that it's preserved for future generations to enjoy."

"But that's hypocritical. Only a very wealthy person could afford to live here."

"True," he admitted readily. "The lots are expensive. The homes people build even more so. But hypocritical? I don't think so.

"With the profits I made on this development I was financially able to provide a sorely needed low-income development close to San Francisco. The people who purchase those homes needed to have housing close to their work. I was able to furnish them with higher-quality homes, carpeted, draped, with built-in appliances, larger rooms, and landscaping at my cost."

"You missed my point," she argued. "These are the people who need this freedom the most."

"I understand. I set aside over three hundred acres of broad beaches and forested meadowland for a campground. I've built camping facilities and offer them free of cost to anyone who needs the tranquillity of this immense coastline to regain his sense of purpose. All I ask is that they respect the land as I do. Fortunately I've had very little vandalism. During the summer I have a constant influx of underprivileged children, Boy Scouts, Camp Fire Girls."

"You're a developer. Why do you feel so strongly about keeping the land in its natural state? The homes are spread out so sparsely."

Leaning back, he tapped his fork against the dish, deep in thought. "My occupation made me aware more than anything could that our modern cities are becoming inhuman. Human beings were not meant to be housed in ugliness and congestion. Each of my developments has parks and is heavily landscaped with trees and grass."

Unaware that he was opening up his innermost thoughts for the first time in his life, he explained readily, "One of man's basic needs is space. You can't walk free in our urban areas. All our movements are governed by endless streams of traffic, all polluting the atmosphere."

His deep insight into problems, his caring for the future generations, added to the respect she had for her dynamic husband.

Leaning forward, he let his elbows rest on the edge of the table. His eyes locked with hers as he continued in a low earnest voice. "With each road that is paved, home built, acre sold, an irrevocable decision is made that affects our future. There are few utopias on this earth. I feel mine is one. This is a vast natural resource along the California coast. The worst crime possible would be desecrating it in such a way that would irreversibly spoil it for our sons and daughters. It's predicted that California will one day be a solid city from San Francisco to San Diego and I'm assuring that my children, as well as others, will have a chance to enjoy land as our forefathers did."

As Derek talked, she took their dishes and empty cups to the double sink of the modern kitchen. Unused to a home built entirely of wood, she found the total effect warm and inviting. Extensive use of glass made each window an invitation to linger, to relax as you watched the changing moods of the surrounding countryside.

Placing the last dish in the cabinet, she suddenly became nervous, knowing they had run out of conversation. The time had come to go to Derek as his wife, to offer her love in hopes of breaking down the final barriers that stood between them and complete contentment.

Head bowed, she gripped the edge of the counter, uncertain what was expected next. The gentle touch of his hands on her shoulders was followed closely by the touch of his lips as he placed his face to her hair.

"You know, don't you?" he whispered slowly before turning her in his arms.

"Yes," she answered softly. "You want me to come to you now as your wife."

"My loving wife," he added unnecessarily.

"You need never doubt that, darling. I've loved you for months." Reaching to him, she was drawn into the comfort of his arms as he swung her off her feet.

With determined strides he carried her from the kitchen, pausing long enough to turn out the light, to their bedroom, whose broad windows looked out on the ocean. The roaring sea's mercurial moods were as varied as the man who built his home on the lonely bluff.

The simple beauty of the heavy wood furniture under the slanted beamed ceiling was as beckoning as the pungent logs burning in the fireplace across from Derek's wide bed. Fog had drifted up from the sea, isolating them in a world of their own.

He set her down, her feet sinking into the thick nap of soft carpeting. Clinging to his waist, she rested her flushed cheeks against the cool silk of his shirt before drawing away.

"Can—can I have some privacy while I bathe?"

"You didn't need any privacy the last time I was in your apartment. You weren't my wife, yet you unhesitantly allowed me to watch you remove your clothes. Were even willing to take off mine. I've dreamed of the pleasures of undressing you myself." Darkened eyes smoldering, he murmured with great feeling, "Would you deny me that satisfaction on my wedding night?"

The look of yearning in his eyes was her undoing and she shook her head. "No, my darling. Tonight I'll deny you nothing." Fingers cradling the lean planes of his beloved face, she raised her lips, yielding all of her abundant love without restraint.

De-Ann felt a shudder run through Derek's body as she touched his lips in a featherlight kiss.

His hands raised to grip her shoulders; his voice sounded thick and ragged. "No kisses yet. I'll be lost if I touch your mouth the way I want to now."

His fingers trembled as he pushed her far enough away to ease the jade-green blazer from her shoulders. It was carelessly cast on the edge of the bedroom chair nearest his side. Both hands untied the bow of her silk blouse after methodically removing her vest.

De-Ann remained still, her breasts rising and falling as she felt his knuckles against the firm sensitive skin. Each button was undone without comment. He unhooked her plaid skirt, removing it effortlessly to join the pile of clothing on the chair.

Derek's eyes turned dark steel-blue and serious, lingering with appreciation on the beauty of her breasts visible beneath the wispy material of her plunging bra. "You're exquisite. My hands are trembling so badly now, I doubt if I'll be able to unhook your bra," he groaned, his voice

196

a throaty murmur in the quiet room. "My stomach's tied in knots just thinking of you beneath me, your naked body mine to hold and give pleasure to."

She stood before him, a soft flush of color touching her cheeks. His blatant declaration of his needs did not surprise her. Thick lashes concealed her own eager anticipation to be his wife.

Derek's hands slid in a caress up her arms to cup her shoulders, his thumbs circling in slow, seductive motions. With a groan he pulled her to the length of his hardened body. "Do you have to bathe first?" His voice was muffled against her neck. Both hands slid down the length of her spine, and he cupped her hips intimately close. The hardness of his body was a potent reminder of the last few months of unaccustomed celibacy.

"I—I would prefer it," she whispered, her voice faltering as she buried her face in the open neckline of his casual shirt. Her arms clasped his waist to steady her trembling body, as always absorbing comfort from his greater strength.

"Too late now!" he blurted out harshly, a strained look on his face. "You smell so sweet and feminine, I'm not waiting any longer. Come to me, my bride. Let me change the look of innocence to awareness. Awareness of the pleasures a man and woman can share."

Derek carried her to his broad bed, reverently lowering her onto the plush coolness of the turned-back sheets. She unhooked her bra and Derek slipped it from her shoulders easily. Her rose-tipped breasts tautened voluptuously beneath his lingering glance. Breathing heavily with anticipation, he trailed his hands over her breasts and abdomen and slipped the sensuous lace briefs from her hips.

De-Ann lay against the earth-toned linens, unashamed of her nudity, her auburn hair splayed over his pillows in a fiery sheen. The love she felt for her husband spilled forth with an unending desire to please him in any way he wished. In the depths of his eyes she could see the pleasure he felt looking at her. They were fine eyes that worshiped with a possessive need to claim her for his personal property.

"I love you, Derek," she whispered poignantly as he stood beside the bed, pulling his knit shirt over his head in one swift motion.

"Good. That will make it easier for you to accept the many intimacies I intend to seek." He casually removed his slacks, then his Jockey shorts.

De-Ann's eyes widened, green as the darkest jade, as she looked at her husband's body for the first time. Stripped, Derek's physical appearance made a startling impact on her senses. His sheer masculine appeal stunned her. He was a giant of a man, bronzed from head to toe with deeply tanned skin. His broad shoulders glistened in the glow of the firelit attic bedroom. His stomach was flat and taut. A black mat of hair curled across his chest with blatant sensuality, forming a narrow strip below his waist. Each muscle was firm and well defined, appealing to her femininity, making her ache to stroke her sensitive fingers over them. She wanted to feel their steel-hard strength and velvety texture with her hands before pressing her body to the length of his in final surrender.

Derek stood motionless, his smoldering eyes lingering on the enticement of her trembling limbs and heaving breasts.

De-Ann knew by the tightly clenched knuckles that his thoughts were troubled, that her husband was still afraid to trust her.

As if he read her mind, his harsh words emphasized her thoughts. "Yes, De-Ann, I am still undecided about your vows to be a faithful, loving wife, but since I paid with my freedom for the right to enjoy the merchandise, I will take

198

the first sample now." Skepticism ate at his mind like acid despite the ache in his heart to give her his complete trust.

"Merchandise!" she spluttered, her temper roused by his harsh sarcasm and continued disbelief. "That's arrogant, uncalled for . . . and cruel." Tears welled in her stormy eyes. Hurt and angry, she jerked upright, intending to leave his house even if she had to walk.

He grabbed her wrist with formidable strength and pulled her beneath the breadth of his chest. His firm mouth easily silenced any further protests.

His lips were insistent, demanding a response yet willing to wait until she relented to their tactile message. His tightly controlled hunger surprised her. Fury abated, she relaxed beneath the seductive pressure. Her lips softened, parting eagerly so he could deepen the kiss.

Derek's mouth left hers to trail across her throat, burning wherever he touched. His lips explored, seeking the vulnerable spot behind her ear, inhaling the sweet perfume of her skin and hair. He took the silky strands into his mouth, tasting them, before traveling down her slender throat to the wildly beating pulse in its hollow. He deliberately sought to arouse her, taking his time, bringing her senses to wild, pulsating life.

De-Ann trembled uncontrollably, biting her lip to stop the plea for him to take her. The aching, felt so often during their stormy courtship, began to increase as his head descended. His name came unbidden, escaping from her lips in breathless whispers as she said over and over, "Derek . . . my darling . . . my love . . . my husband."

She had neither the desire nor the ability to control her craving for his continued stimulation. The urge for fulfillment aroused by his ceaseless caressing touch was a wondrous experience.

Derek mastered De-Ann's emotions totally. His years of experience had evolved into an expertise of sexual dominance that was beyond her most vivid fantasies. Her passionate response inflamed him as he kept his desire to take her quickly under control.

Wave after wave of erotic pleasure surged through her writhing body. Any previous vow to give him her love without restraint was unnecessary. Derek's personality would not tolerate a lukewarm response. His seduction would not be complete until her pent-up longings equaled his. She was on fire for him and he knew it.

His lips hungrily reclaimed her mouth in a seemingly endless kiss. She lay gasping for some semblance of composure as he nibbled each side of her soft pulsating lips before moving over her cheeks. His hands were relentless, stroking, lingering, and stroking again on each curve of her quivering body.

His voice thickened, love words coming unbidden, murmured raggedly against her skin. "Umm . . . so soft and silky. So beautifully responsive and passionate to my touch . . ." His speech became incoherent, broken off as his tongue flicked against her neck, the need to taste her delectable skin unbearable. He circled her inner ear, probing until she clung to his nape, fingers entangled in his hair.

Cupping one full breast in his palm, he sought the delicate pink tip. It hardened instantly to a taut bud beneath his tongue. "So good. So very, very good," he moaned, before burying his face against the full rounded curve. His moist sucking motions caused her stomach to clench in tight knots, demanding satisfaction.

De-Ann's fingers clung, released, and clung again before sliding across his shoulders. She arched her body upward, instinctively pushing sideways to get under his hips, her smooth thigh moving over his hair-roughened leg in an attempt to get closer. She moved restlessly, each touch more arousing than the one before.

Derek eased her onto her back again, his mouth leaving her breast only long enough to command, "Lie still! I'm not finished loving you this way yet." His voice was ragged, barely recognizable, from his tormented need for relief.

He gave her throbbing breasts a lingering flick across the nipples before moving down, intent on probing each tantalizing portion of her satin-smooth anatomy. His hands were gentle as they parted her thighs, then moved upward to caress her body's most sensitive area until she arched to meet the pressure of his hand, seeking satisfaction. Unbidden murmurs of intense pleasure came from her throat, tiny whimpering pleas for release from his stimulating touch.

So expert was Derek's tutoring, De-Ann made no protest when his mouth lowered across her abdomen. Her heart hammered expectantly, body arching and pliant beneath him as he placed kisses along the length of each trembling leg. Outer thigh to back of knee and down to the smooth soles of her feet, before returning a different path along the inner leg. Ever upward his lips caressed her, to the top of her velvety limbs until she lay trembling beneath his searching, restless tongue as wave after wave of sexual pleasure seared the apex of her sensitive femininity.

Derek knew she was ready when he placed his body between her parted thighs. She was filled with the warmth of his love. Eager, she squirmed, arching so they could cleave as one. The giving and receiving touched her with wonder to the depths of her soul. Her heart overflowed with love for her tempestuous husband.

Muffled beneath his seeking mouth, her smothered cry was short when the first penetration with his thrusting body took her final innocence. She never flinched, her hips raised to accept his entry joyously, fingers clinging to his back with each deepening movement.

"I love you, my darling. Forever and ever," she cried out.

On and on he continued until her body was rocked by explosive shock waves, one after the other. The new sensation was strange to her but more pleasurable than any she had ever known. She knew from his husky moans that Derek, too, felt the same.

The satisfaction and beauty of their first love had exceeded her wildest visions. She lay indolently within his arms, her eyes luminous pools of brilliant jade lingering on her husband's beloved face. He withdrew his weight to enable his hands to slide with great reverence over her satiated body, still flushed from his ardent lovemaking.

God, he loved her. She was his very breath of life, he thought. She had denied him nothing. Had allowed him total succor in expressing his love, despite her naiveté. Until their coming together with love, Derek had foolishly believed all women—any woman—were much the same.

Yet years of deeply ingrained cynicism warred with his love. Smoldering distrust ate at the knowledge that she was now his, despite his having known he was her first lover. Her virtuous love was given with such uninhibited joy, he felt remorse and unbearable guilt, as she lay clinging to him in the aftermath of passion.

Unaware of Derek's troubled thoughts, De-Ann lay her head on his chest. One soft hand caressed his strong jaw, while her low murmurs of love echoed in the silent room, her need for his touch as slow to die as the embers of the waning fire.

CHAPTER ELEVEN

De-Ann woke slowly. A deep sense of lethargy filled her body, utter contentment bringing a soft flush to her cheeks. Eyelids heavy with sleep, she murmured huskily. Reaching for Derek, her groping hands touched cool empty sheets. Bereft of her husband's warmth, she sat up alarmed.

The instinctive knowledge that Derek had left brought a cry to her lips. Rushing to the closet for a wraparound robe, she felt heat touch her cheeks, knowing she had not worn the nightgown and peignoir still hanging in their closet.

Distracted in her haste to find out what had caused Derek to leave, she nearly missed his note. It sat propped on the heavy dresser across the room. She walked forward, pulse beating frantically, fingers trembling. As she read it her heart plummeted with despair.

My darling wife,
Though it tears my heart, I had to leave you. The giving of your first love so freely, with such uninhibit-

ed passion, has filled me with guilt. Guilt because I dared distrust you. Remorse because cynicism still torments my thoughts.

It's imperative to our future happiness that I rid myself of the feeling that your devotion will not last.

Forgive me for sneaking away like a thief in the night. I knew if I woke with you in my arms, you'd be hurt by my doubts over your vows of fidelity.

I love you.

Derek

Tears blurred her vision when she reached the end of his heartrending note. Each word filled her mind with anguish. She knew the torment that had driven him to leave her after long hours of tender lovemaking was not of his making. The blame rested solely with the instability of his young mother and transferred bitterness of his father. His stepmother's blatant advances had come at a time when he was emotionally still an immature youth. The shock had left deep, permanent scars of distrust.

With his note crushed to her breast De-Ann walked to the front of their loft bedroom and sat on a wide window seat. Curling her bare feet beneath her on the soft cushion, she leaned against the alcove wall, built to overlook the turbulent ocean.

Keeping her eyes from the rumpled covers of the mammoth bed where they had shared long hours of tumultuous lovemaking, she watched the fog lift in the early-morning light. It left its dampness on blades of meadow grass and thin needles of windswept cypress hedgerows, which added a fresh sparkle to the beginning of a new day.

Tears started to fall unchecked down her cheeks. Her mother's warning came unbidden, reminding her that Derek needed a gentle touch, that she should be prepared for a turbulent beginning.

"Oh, my darling!" she cried out to the empty room. "I was so certain I had convinced you of my eternal love."

She knew Derek could never doubt he had been her first lover. The evidence of her purity was obvious up to the moment she received him with eagerness into her body.

Hands trembling, she reread his note before folding it to place in the recesses of her purse. She sighed, knowing she was partially to blame with her foolish attempts to deceive him. A sudden inner strength filled her with peace. Derek would return in his own time.

"I'll be waiting, my love. For always," she whispered.

Used to leading an active life, De-Ann rose. The days would be full until her husband returned. She vowed he wouldn't find her moping or depressed. She'd welcome his return with open arms and a smile on her lips.

Upon returning to their bedroom, she gathered a pair of brown designer jeans and a turtleneck sweater in soft tan. With clean underwear she placed them on the edge of the bed before entering the adjoining master bath.

Slipping the robe from her shoulders, she stood before the mirrored wall, her reflection showing in sharp detail. De-Ann was amazed—her body was still faintly flushed with the aftermath of their passionate lovemaking. But otherwise she looked the same.

"Such a traumatic event in my life should be noticeable," she complained jokingly to her image. Other than the shining awareness in the depths of her eyes, there was no visible sign that she had passed the barriers of innocence.

Every place Derek's gentle touch had lingered seemed to throb with new sensitivity. An experienced, confident lover, he had seduced her slowly despite the obviousness of his aroused masculinity. His urgent desire to take her hastily had been tamped until he was certain she could reach a climax of sensual excitement equal to his.

Adjusting the water to the correct temperature, De-Ann stepped into the tiled stall shower, which had been sized to comfortably hold Derek's brawny frame. Last night he had pulled her inside as they cleansed their heated bodies. A vain attempt, she thought, remembering the erotic feel of their sleek bodies clasped in passionate embrace beneath the cool spray.

De-Ann turned to let the spray rinse the suds from her shoulders. Her breasts, still sensitive from his ardent lovemaking, tingled beneath the fine mist. Sudden need flowed through her veins, causing her limbs to tremble as she soaped her flat stomach downward to her thighs.

Derek had been right, she thought, when he told her she would be unhappy living a sexually baren life once she was awakened. One night of his torrid caresses and she ached to experience them over and over again.

A potent lover, Derek had caressed her with unhurried strokes. His virile demands were relentless, but she met each request eagerly. Exalting in his dominant commands for reciprocation, she willingly followed his lead. Giving him pleasure was her final transformation into womanhood.

Before falling asleep with the satisfying exhaustion of total sexual gratification, she had been made aware—with tender, exploring hands and warm, caressing lips—of the sensitivity of her entire trembling body. Uninhibited in her desire to please, she had returned each touch with a caress of her own.

Derek's delight in her fiery response was obvious. She had clasped his shuddering body time after time. Clinging to the steel-hard muscles of his back, her caressing hands had drawn him closer, their breaths intermingling during the exchange of fervent vows of devotion.

She remembering his wedding day admonition and a smile touched her mouth. Long before the bedroom clock chimed midnight, her claims of virginity were no longer valid.

Forcing her thoughts from the complexities of her husband's personality and extreme virility, she spent long hours exploring her new home. The breathtaking beauty of the cliff-top setting was an ever-changing enchantment.

One day passed to the next. A routine was soon established. After straightening her home she would spend the daylight hours investigating the many delights of Hidden Coves. She walked the winding roadway to the complex center. The rustic weathered shops nestled unobtrusively near the main highway. Lodge, restaurant, market, and sales offices all appeared to bustle with activity.

De-Ann introduced herself to the curious staff and they soon became friends. She would listen with pride as they extolled the generosity of her husband.

Insight to her husband's character was gained when she studied the restrictions he imposed to protect the spectacular natural attractions of Hidden Coves. Utilities were underground. No fences were allowed to mar the landscape. Architecture varied. Houses were designed to harmonize with the coastal setting. Each one had been sided with redwood and would eventually weather to the same pastoral gray.

Each day De-Ann scrambled down the steep cliffs along an access she had picked out among the rocks. She remembered Derek's warning to be careful of the tides so she checked them carefully before walking along the rugged coastline.

Each evening before dark she would return home, cheeks flushed a healthy pink, silky hair tumbled about her slender shoulders. Living in blue jeans, pullover sweaters, and tennis shoes, she couldn't remember a time in her adult life when she had been more content. The only mar was Derek's continued absence.

Her busy days did not tire her, instead they invigorated her. Filled with abundant energy, she spent part of her evenings cooking in the comfortable kitchen. Tensions had been released numerous times standing at the wooden chopping block, vigorously kneading yeasty bread dough. The large deep freezer was nearly filled with home-baked bread, cakes, cookies, and pies.

Her favorite spot was the wide windowseat under the slanted beams of their loft bedroom. A powerful telescope, which had been placed in front of the windows on permanent mountings, provided her with hours of enchantment. The search for fat California sea lions and harbor seals had been successful, but disappointment plagued her at missing the annual migration of the majestic gray whale.

Cormorants flew daily, bodies outstretched directly over the ocean. Comical-looking brown pelicans dove for fish, followed by screeching sea gulls waiting for a free meal. Hawks, doves, and quail were plentiful.

After a while, though, De-Ann longed to do some creative work. During a trip to the complex center she asked one of her new friends to call Derek's San Francisco home and have Smitty and Charlie send her some of her basic art supplies. By the end of the week she had completed the preliminary illustrations and the gothic lettering for Mr. Percy's children's book and mailed it, hoping it would meet his approval. In her spare hours, as she sat in the sunshine, overlooking the roaring ocean, she wrote thank-you cards to the generous guests at her and Derek's wedding, including a personal note to those she especially remembered.

De-Ann's need for artistic expression was helped by a fall she took while searching tidepools for sea anemones. She had worn a suede jacket to keep out the early-morning chill, and the sharp rocks had cut an irreparable tear across the front. She carefully cut the unseamed back from its lining and laid it smoothly over the kitchen table.

Each evening she worked on the soft suede with short deft strokes. The love in her heart flowed through the ability of her fingers until the image she was seeking stared back, indelibly drawn with black ink.

Recalling the scandal sheet's words—"Ms. De-Ann Wagner seems to have penned her man with permanent ink"—she chuckled out loud. They were right, after all, she thought as she admired her completed work.

Derek's forceful features stared at her. His rough-cut raven hair tumbled across the top of his forehead in disarray. Eyes so lifelike they seemed to follow her watched from the taut contours of his face. His strong chin jutted forward, giving a clear impression of character and strength.

A touch of mischief had caused her to raise the corners of his lips into a half-smile. His image was reproduced exactly as he had looked when he had stood on the windy bluff to show her the view the day of their marriage.

Returning from an early-morning walk along the top of the cliffs in front of their home, De-Ann looked toward the sun to see the brawny image of a man. Legs splayed, hands on hips, he watched her approach, standing in the shadow of his friend's house.

Her cry of delight was caught by the breeze but she ran forward, arms outstretched to enfold her husband's waist. "Derek . . . Derek! Oh, my darling. . . . I've missed you so. . . ."

She stopped abruptly, her words of love broken off, when she realized the man looming before her wasn't Derek. Tears streamed down her cheeks as she held her bowed head in trembling hands. Overcome with grief and disappointment, she cried without shame.

The stranger spoke, his deep voice uncertain as he tried

to bring her comfort. Touching her shoulder, he pleaded, "Please, don't cry."

Taking a handkerchief from the pocket of her blue jeans, she turned to wipe her eyes. When she regained control, she faced him, her reddened eyes and quivering chin the only sign of distress.

"Are you looking for Derek?"

"Yes. I'm Sasq O'Brien. I hoped to talk with Derek while I'm here. You are . . . ?" he questioned curiously.

"Mrs. Derek!" she teased, laughing at his shocked expression. "Call me De-Ann." Placing her small hand in his calloused palm, she apologized for her behavior. "I can see you're as surprised as his other friends to see that Derek married."

De-Ann invited him in for a cup of coffee, and when they reached the house, she excused herself. After washing her hands and applying fresh makeup, she felt better. Entering the kitchen where Sasq was sitting at the kitchen table, she reached for the percolator.

"Did you do this, De-Ann?" he asked, looking at the suede picture of Derek before she moved it aside.

"Yes. Derek's working in Spain and I needed to keep busy in my spare time," she lied.

"Do you think it looks like my husband?" she asked, placing a mug of steaming coffee and a wedge of chocolate cake in front of him.

"A perfect image of the man. Rather arrogant with a touch of humor. Most definitely drawn by a woman very much in love with her subject."

"Does it show that much?" she asked, sipping the strong brew as she sat across from Derek's friend.

"In the picture very much but even more so from your face when you realized that I wasn't your husband."

"You and he look astonishingly alike from a distance.

The sun blinded me, plus I wasn't expecting anyone but Derek to appear."

Refilling his cup before slicing another piece of cake and handing it to him, she knew she had found a friend. His keen eyes, though filled with admiration, were not those of a man seeking a romantic interest.

Much the same size as Derek, he had the same midnight-black hair. Where Derek's eyes were deep blue, Sasq's were black. His strong chin was covered with several days' growth of beard.

Noticing her gaze on his jaw, he reached up to rub it with his hand. "Pretty scruffy-looking, isn't it? I have a legitimate reason for letting it grow, other than laziness," he teased, feeling De-Ann's need for platonic friendship.

"Actually, Sasq, you look like my idea of a lumberjack. With your red and black shirt and slim-legged jeans I can picture you with an ax over your shoulder."

"You hit the nail on the head, De-Ann. Lumber is my living. That's how I met Derek. He came to my company nursery to buy hundreds of seedlings for this development. Many of the Monterey cypress, Douglas fir, giant fir, redwood and Bishop pine growing here so profusely as windbreaks were planted by your husband."

"How interesting. Do you live near here, Sasq?"

"No. I'm from the deep woods farther north. I flew in yesterday on business. I'll be staying at Derek's lodge for a few days."

"Are you married?" she asked inquisitively. De-Ann guessed he would never lack female companionship.

"No. I haven't met my woman yet, but like Derek I'll not waste time when I find her." His black eyes glimmered with amusement but his tone was serious. A deep voice that, like her husband's, held authority.

"Your name is so unusual. Does it have a special meaning?"

"Yes. It's pronounced Sask but spelled with a *Q* and is short for Sasquatch."

"You mean like the Indian word for Bigfoot?" De-Ann asked curiously, having read several articles on the legendary creature.

"The same. My mother was one-fourth Indian and my father one-hundred-percent Irish. When I was born, I had so much dark hair that Dad called me Sasquatch. Sasquatch Timothy O'Brien. Quite some handle, isn't it?" Suddenly serious, he said, "Tell me why you looked so sad before, De-Ann."

His large sun-bronzed hand cupped a mug of hot coffee as he listened with sympathy to De-Ann's problem. He admired the independence and inherent pride that made her wait without complaint until Derek found release from the scars of his past.

De-Ann finished with a big sigh of relief. Some of the pain was eased by sharing her turmoil with Derek's friend.

His jet-black eyes were filled with compassion. Thanking her for the cake, coffee, and confidences, he left.

Each day throughout the week De-Ann and Sasq met. As they walked through the meadowlands he pointed out numerous varieties of plant life and wild creatures, identifying each one matter-of-factly. A true man of nature. She found his company soothing, his appreciation of the natural environment equal to Derek's.

In the evenings they ate simple home-cooked meals together. Soon their friendship became a strong bond, the exchange of confidences a solace.

Sasq offered to make a frame for Derek's picture and mount it for her. The polished redwood frame matched the furnishings in their secluded bedroom. De-Ann hung it above the fireplace mantel, where she could see it from every corner, his image helping her retain her rapidly decreasing composure.

Marking off the days, she suddenly found it necessary to force down the restlessness building up inside her body. Sleep was increasingly difficult. Discontented fretting had developed into a weary habit.

Another week started with no word from Derek. DeAnn sighed with dejection after a long sleepless night. She knelt by the alcove to look out the window. The sky was filled with steely gray clouds that matched the surging ocean.

"Even the weather's gloomy," she complained aloud. "Matches my mood exactly."

Knowing Sasq would be busy with meetings all day added to her misery. She would miss him. He was a good listener, never interrupting, though she knew he had to be tired of hearing about her love for Derek.

Pulling a pair of snug-fitting jeans over her hips, she noticed the waistband was looser. "Damn it, now I'm starting to lose weight. Derek Howell, you darn well better get back here to your lonesome wife!" she grumbled mutinously.

Voice muffled by the brown long-sleeve turtleneck sweater being pulled over her head, she spoke grimly. "My vow to greet you with open arms may be changed to welcoming you with a rolling pin off your stubborn head!"

After a breakfast of steaming hot coffee and the toasted heel of homemade bread, she decided to do some baking, then take her hike in the afternoon.

In a whirl of activity she mixed the batter for two fat loaves of bread, kneaded it, and placed it in a large greased bowl with a damp cloth over the top to rise.

Taking half a dozen crisp, juicy pippin apples, she propped herself on a kitchen stool to peel the skins in long strips. A gift from the complex gardener, they were the first of the season, picked from his home orchard. As she made the apple pie the aroma pervaded the kitchen, the sharp cinnamon blending with the sweet apple.

By the time her pie and bread had baked, she had changed the bed linens, cleaned the bathroom, shined and polished every room until it glistened.

After working nonstop all morning, she took a walk and gathered interesting leaves and assorted-size pine cones. Arranging them skillfully in a low woven basket, she set them in the center of the broad coffee table in front of the couch.

Many changes had been made since she had been isolated. While rummaging through closets, she had found attractive vases, pillows, new linens and towels, canisters and copper pans for the kitchen. Letting her imagination run free, she had transformed his bare home, adding her personal touch to each room.

In the afternoon, feeling a need for the outdoors, she grabbed a crisp apple, zipped her red windbreaker high to her throat to keep out the wind, and walked to the edge of the cliff. She scampered fearlessly down its near vertical face, even leaped the last three feet to the sand, to explore the tidepools.

Sheltered from the fierce winds at the base of the cliffs, she removed her jacket, placing it on a large rock. Her teeth sank into the crisp apple, each bite juicy, as she wandered head down along the shallow beach.

The small sea creatures visible in the clear saltwater enchanted her. Continuing on to previously unexplored shoreline, she found a small cove with soft white sand. She sat below the steep cliffs, her arms around bent knees.

She watched entranced as giant breakers slammed against the rocks that jutted up from the ocean floor before her. Fog was creeping in, covering the horizon completely. The sun, totally obliterated by the dark sky, gave no warmth.

Curling in the soft sand, De-Ann shut her eyes, relaxing after her morning's activities. Nights of sleeplessness took their toll, and she drifted into a deep sleep, lulled by the steady ebb and flow of the surf.

Cold and stiff, De-Ann woke with a start. She looked with alarm as an incoming wave delivered a swath of foam at her feet. Derek's warning had gone unheeded—she had forgotten to check the tides.

The rocks she had scampered over to reach the cove were now covered by water. Her only exit was the cliff face. Searching frantically for a foothold, she cried out with fear. She was trapped in the tiny cove by her own carelessness. Panic filled her mind as she turned to watch the surging ocean, each wave closer than the one before. Hypnotized by fear, she stood motionless against the face of the cliff, unaware of her desperate cries for her husband.

Arriving home, Derek gave a cursory search through his home for De-Ann. Eager to find his bride, he barely noticed the imprint of her personality on his home. He knew she wasn't at the complex center, but he was unable to understand her being out in such blustery weather. Rain was threatening to start any moment and the sky was turning black as night. He felt terror touch his nape. With psychic perception he knew his beloved wife was in desperate trouble.

He rushed to the edge of the cliff, fear mounting. He looked to the south, horror making him break out in a cold sweat—De-Ann's red Windbreaker was floating in and out with the tide.

Hearing his name called, he looked up to see Sasq O'-Brien rushing toward him.

Derek yelled "It's De-Ann," without preamble. "Some-things wrong. I can't find her."

Used to handling emergencies, as was Derek, he motioned he would check the cliffs to the south while Derek searched north. Derek's long strides carried him close to the dangerous edge of the cliffs, but he didn't dare let himself think of the possibility of De-Ann's slender body pounded against the rocks. She would be helpless if caught in the inrushing tide.

Suddenly he heard a frantic screech, his name called in a hoarse, pain-filled cry. Leaning over the edge, he saw her standing in waist-deep swirling water. Below him was seventy-five feet of sheer cliff.

Having found no trace at the south end, Sasq arrived breathlessly. He heard the cries and ran to Derek.

Derek's curt orders to go to his garage and get rope were heeded. "I'm going down."

"My God, man, you'll be killed. The cliff's too steep," Sasq yelled to stop him.

"If I don't, she'll die. If she does, I do too. Go!"

After checking the edge for the best spot, Derek slithered down, stopped by a brief rocky ledge jutting out. Without thought for his own safety he managed to find tiny footholds, his palms clinging to the rough cliff face. Sweat dripped from his pores, each second seemed like an eternity. Not daring to look down, he prayed De-Ann would be safe until he reached her.

His weeks without her had taught him that life had no meaning unless she was at his side. As the rocks slipped beneath his feet, he could hear them cascade over the precipitous cliff into the surf.

Aware for the first time that Derek was coming to her, De-Ann turned to face the cliff, arms reaching high over her head. She waited, certain Derek would rescue her.

Derek slid the last few feet to a ledge above De-Ann's head. Aware that the tide was becoming more violent, he knew what he had to do. He jumped into the ocean, and when he surfaced, he grabbed her waist, raising her out of

216

the water until she stood trembling and quiet on the small ledge.

Slipping on the steep, wet cliff face, Derek finally managed to pull himself upward. His physical strength and natural agility saved his life as a crashing wave broke below them.

Arms wrapped around De-Ann, he held her close against the bluff, assessing a safe route to take to the top. He wondered if she would be able to make it: she was so cold and frightened.

He heard Sasq's call and sighed with relief as a sturdy nylon rope was dropped over the edge. Derek tied a knot around De-Ann's waist, then called to Sasq to pull.

Long torturous minutes passed as Derek scrambled up the slippery cliff, pushing De-Ann before him, the climb made possible by the assistance of Sasq's pull of the rope.

Once they were over the edge, De-Ann lay silent, resting on the cliff top. Derek lay alongside her, his arm thrown over her protectively while he regained his breath.

Long moments passed before he rose, cradling her trembling body in his gentle arms. With long strides the two men walked toward Derek's home.

De-Ann felt her panic leave as she nestled in the safety of her husband's broad body. Teeth chattering, she whispered against his neck, "I'm . . . I'm . . . okay. You . . . you . . . saved my life."

Without looking at her, he continued across the rough grass, rain pelting their faces as the heavens opened up. "Hush now."

Arriving at his home, Derek kicked the door shut behind him after assuring Sasq they would both be fine. No thanks were needed now. They could be given after Derek saw to his wife's comfort.

He carried her straight to their bathroom and set her on her feet. With gentle hands he stripped the soaked clothes from her body. Awe-struck by his arrival, she stood silent, tears of thankfulness trailing down her cheeks in a steady stream.

Derek pushed her inside the shower, anxious to get the chill from her body. He, too, stripped and stepped inside. After they were both clean, he gathered her into his arms for the first time, his great body shuddering at the thought of her close call with death.

Slender arms wrapped around Derek's neck, De-Ann raised her lips to meet his mouth, the touch so intense, she whimpered uncontrollably. Stepping from the shower, he dried her flushed body before wrapping her in the warm folds of his velour robe. Its huge size dwarfing her, she padded into their bedroom.

Derek lit a fire and it blazed quickly, giving added warmth to the room. Flashes of lightning could be seen outside the wide window as rain pounded the heavy wood shingles of the steep roof with relentless persistence.

Safe and warm inside their home, De-Ann watched as Derek stood before the glowing fire. She ran forward, arms outstretched, to cradle him inside the folds of the robe. Their naked bodies clung as his towel fell unnoticed to the rug. He pushed the robe off her shoulders, lifted her into his arms, and lay her carefully on the fresh sheets.

The pungent odor of burning logs permeated the room with a woodsy smell. Uncaring, he inhaled his wife's scent, burying his face reverently in her tousled hair. His long frame stretched beneath the covers, moving closer to hers.

Trembling at the near loss of his wife, Derek needed constant reassurance that she was safe. With a sense of urgency he cupped her supple body beneath him, moans of desire escaping his throat before his mouth clung to the sweetness of her parted lips. Terror filled him at the faint taste of salty ocean spray that still clung to her skin.

Fervent words were whispered against her lips between deep hungering kisses.

De-Ann's heart filled with peace hearing Derek thank God for her protection. Her husband had come to her with trust. Any lingering doubts that she would deceive him had been washed away as surely as the surging ocean washed against the sandy shore.

Cradling his head, she felt blood roar through her veins as he plundered the side of her neck with fervent caresses. He tasted each delectable inch of silky skin. Her body trembled convulsively, arching upward as he reached the taut curves of her breasts, tips stirred to erectness.

Familiar now with knowledge of sexual fulfillment, De-Ann responded quickly, holding his head with trembling fingers as he worshiped the mature roundness of her swollen breasts. The warmth of his mouth surging against her sensitive nipples caused her to cry out with desire.

Moving beneath his aroused body, she parted her thighs from the hardness of his entwined limbs. As her fingers clung to the solid muscles of his broad shoulders, her hips raised instinctively, seeking the sensual satisfaction he had taught her to crave. Out of breath, eyes luminous with desire, she beseeched him to take her, her soft body a pale contrast to his hard bronze torso.

"But you're not ready," he groaned, his husky voice barely audible.

"I'll always be ready for you, my husband," she whispered.

Unable to resist her plea, he possessed her, their passion as wild as the storm that raged outside their home.

Nails digging into his broad back, De-Ann cried out. Derek's fierce lovemaking was so ardent, she felt she would die with sheer pleasure as they simultaneously reached a shattering climax.

Spent, they lay quiet, bodies slowly relaxing from the turmoil of their rapturous coming together.

Lying on his back, Derek cradled her with his right arm, his lean hand stroking her damp hair, sensuous mouth placing lazy kisses to her forehead between whispered words of love.

Lips pressed against his chest, De-Ann inhaled the scent of her husband's clean body, his warmth filling her with contentment. She twined her fingers in the mat of dark hair covering his heart. At ease in their intimacy, she allowed her hand to trace the hair down to the flatness of his abdomen and below.

He raised his hand to stop her stroking and held hers over his stomach while they shared confidences.

De-Ann, snuggled lazily next to her husband's side, listened as he explained the struggle he had had to rid his mind of the suspicions and cynicism.

Filled with guilt for his lack of faith in his new wife, he had driven to San Francisco, spending hours talking with her mother, explaining his reasons for leaving her daughter. Mrs. Wagner's assurances of caring without reproach had made a deep impression. For the first time he realized the foolishness of doubting De-Ann.

Next he had flown to Spain to complete the project he had started and while there he visited with Nick and Carlyn. Unlike De-Ann's mother's soft-spoken advice Nick had criticized him vehemently.

Derek placed a swift kiss to his wife's parted lips. Glancing at his picture above the fireplace, he told her softly, "If all my advice hadn't convinced me, that would have. Will you sketch me a matching self-portrait so I'll have something beautiful to look at when I wake up?"

"I most certainly will not!" she scolded impudently. "If you want to look at me, you can do it in bed!"

Glancing down the length of her soft body, Derek let his

eyes linger on the beauty of her naked breasts before lowering slowly to stare at each exquisite portion exposed to his gaze.

De-Ann caressed him as she watched his expression change from lazy indulgence to a smoldering warning.

"My libido has a hair trigger with you, so be prepared to pay the consequences if your fingers become any bolder."

Eyes alight with mischief, she moved her hands deliberately lower.

With alarming quickness, Derek rolled her onto her back. Pinning her wrists on each side of her face, he watched her eyes soften. Her hair, tumbled from their earlier passion, spread over the pillow, its color as fiery as the flames from the burning logs. Lips parting invitingly, she smiled.

"Can I love you, my wife?" he whispered, the touch of his clean breath soft on her face.

"One time only, my husband," she teased softly, arms pulling free to clasp his neck, fingers stroking his raven-black hair.

"One won't do, my darling. . . . One won't do!"

Dell Bestsellers

- [ ] **NOBLE HOUSE** by James Clavell $5.95 (16483-4)
- [ ] **PAPER MONEY** by Adam Smith $3.95 (16891-0)
- [ ] **CATHEDRAL** by Nelson De Mille $3.95 (11620-1)
- [ ] **YANKEE** by Dana Fuller Ross $3.50 (19841-0)
- [ ] **LOVE, DAD** by Evan Hunter $3.95 (14998-3)
- [ ] **WILD WIND WESTWARD**
  by Vanessa Royal $3.50 (19363-X)
- [ ] **A PERFECT STRANGER**
  by Danielle Steel $3.50 (17221-7)
- [ ] **FEED YOUR KIDS RIGHT**
  by Lendon Smith, M.D. $3.50 (12706-8)
- [ ] **THE FOUNDING**
  by Cynthia Harrod-Eagles $3.50 (12677-0)
- [ ] **GOODBYE, DARKNESS**
  by William Manchester $3.95 (13110-3)
- [ ] **GENESIS** by W.A. Harbinson $3.50 (12832-3)
- [ ] **FAULT LINES** by James Carroll $3.50 (12436-0)
- [ ] **MORTAL FRIENDS** by James Carroll $3.95 (15790-0)
- [ ] **THE SOLID GOLD CIRCLE**
  by Sheila Schwartz $3.50 (18156-9)
- [ ] **AMERICAN CAESAR**
  by William Manchester $4.50 (10424-6)

At your local bookstore or use this handy coupon for ordering:

DELL BOOKS
P.O. BOX 1000, PINE BROOK, N.J. 07058-1000

Please send me the books I have checked above. I am enclosing $ _____ (please add 75c per copy to cover postage and handling). Send check or money order—no cash or C.O.D.'s. Please allow up to 8 weeks for shipment.

Mr./Mrs./Miss _____

Address _____

City _____ State/Zip _____